Without Warning

Mike Smart

The moral right of the author has been asserted

To our friends and family

thank you for all your support and encouragement to

Get On With It

Prologue

Disputed lands – Fifteen Years Earlier

The young boy looked into the lifeless eyes of his father; he would never forget that sight nor the putrid smell of his beloved parents' now-emptied bowels. He had held his father's hand as the final signs of life had ebbed away unable to stem the bleeding caused by the shrapnel which had ripped through his body. It didn't seem right that the man who had brought him to life, had fed him and cared for their family should have spent his last few minutes on earth wracked in pain and laying in the dirt stained with his own urine and faeces.

He looked across at where his older sister and mother lay. The whole family had been working in their small field trying to scrape some sort of a life from the hard unforgiving land. There had been no warning, no indication that the lives of his immediate family would so suddenly and violently be cut short.

On that fateful day, their incessant toiling had been made that much harder by the hot morning sun beating down. They had been working together for a couple of hours before his father had instructed him to go to the village well and bring back two goat skin pouches full of cold refreshing water. As he had walked back up the small path, up the steep incline back to the plot of land they called their own, he had seen wisps of vapour trail in the azure sky. He had stopped, shielding his eyes to get a better look at these miracles in the air. It was always a great source of amazement to him, a poorly educated boy, how these planes ever managed to stay in the sky. He often wondered what it might be like to fly. Where were they from and where were they going? This was one of his favourite guessing games to play silently in his head.

The noise had been deafening as the high explosive bombs had gone off a quarter of a mile away from where he stood. The earth had shook and he had immediately thrown himself to the ground in a mixture of fright and pure shock. As he had hit the hard-baked dried earth he knew at once that the bomb, or bombs, would have landed close to where his family had been working.

Picking himself up off the floor, he had left the now-forgotten water sacks behind him as he had raced up the slope towards where his family should have been waiting for him.

At 20,000 ft no one in the American B52 bomber had felt the shock waves from the explosions from far below and the crew had carried on happily chatting away. They had been given their coordinates and done their job little knowing that they had inadvertently dropped their payload in the wrong place. Not only had they killed several, totally innocent noncombatants, but they had also spawned a radical of the worst sort. No home, no family, no great cause; this young man had nothing left to lose and had just inherited a lifelong desire to inflict as much pain and suffering as possible on those that had destroyed all that had mattered to him.

He had made a vow at the very moment of his father's passing that his own life was forfeit and that all he should focus on henceforth was to bring death and destruction to the people that had come unwanted into his land. The uninvited foreigners hadn't come to grant the indigenous tribes freedom but to help keep them oppressed. Well, he would make sure that the three 'superpowers' which made up the bulk of the coalition forces would never forget this day.

Hamburg, Germany – Friday, Early Morning

Max woke with a fitful start; the oversized hotel bed was damp, soaked through with his sweat. It had been another bad night's sleep, the image of watching Clare being crushed under thousands of tons of masonry etched forever more into his optic nerves. He rolled over and checked his dive watch 03.20. The meeting wasn't for another five hours odd. Closing his eyes, he tried to will himself to sleep. 04.05, 04.26 ... slipped by all too slowly.

He climbed out of bed and decided that he wasn't going to be able to get back to sleep. He turned on the main room lights, visited the bathroom and then came back into the main room to do a few warm up stretching exercises. Dropping to the floor, he then focused on his morning workout of press ups and sit ups. Twenty minutes later he had exited the hotel, which was positioned on the edge of the Aussenalster, wearing his favoured tracksuit bottoms, a well-worn T-shirt and a heavy sweatshirt to help fend off the bitter German cold air. It was still dark at this time of the morning but his way was well lit by the abundance of street lighting.

Cutting across the four lane road he jogged down to the edge of the outer of two lakes which forms part of the very attractive backdrop to Hamburg's central shopping district. He turned left and jogged at a steady rate, crossing the Kennedybruecke and Lombardsbruecke in turn. He was now running along the Binnenalster; to his right he could see the fountain that shot water hundred and fifty feet into the air. The scene always reminded him of Geneva.

There were only a few other hardy souls out at that time of day; the rush hour wouldn't start in earnest for another hour or so. The run was doing him good, he had a hard day ahead of him and he used the time as he ran to think about the confrontation that lay ahead. His route took him through the deserted shopping streets down to the Elbe River at Landungsbruecken. Hamburg is a beautiful city, many of the finest old buildings having been painstakingly rebuilt after the terrible damage wrought by the bombings inflicted on the city during the second world war. Max had slowed a little to look in some of the shop windows as he made his way through the network of streets crisscrossing a couple of small canals which joined the lakes with the river. *No recession here*, he thought.

He knew Hamburg pretty well, and having made the turning point of his run at the ferry terminus at Landungsbruecken he made his way back up the fairly steep climb to St Michael's Cathedral and back towards the far side of the inner Alster. By the time he got back to his room he'd worked up a good sweat and thoroughly enjoyed the drenching shower in his smart ensuite bathroom.

~

"Dieter, my name is Max Thatcher." He was standing in front of a desk in a small, very expensively decorated office just off the infamous Reeperbahn situated in the less than salubrious district of Hamburg known as St Pauli's. The area was famous for all sorts of things but most notably as a red light district and the venue for the historic Beetles concert that set them on their way. Set between the river and the main centre of Hamburg, it had been a favourite place for merchant seaman to spend a night of debauchery. It was less frequented by visiting sailors these days as Hamburg's status as a Hanseatic port was more a point of historical interest than of commercial import. The shortfall of visitors from the sea was now more than made up for by the huge number of tourists who liked the pristine side of Hamburg but couldn't resist seeing the seedier side at the same time. It had become a great tourist trap, full of bars and nightclubs, one street still set aside for stag groups to go and view naked women in the shop windows and venture in if they dare. On the face of it the area was probably safer than it used to be for the unwary, but there was still a palpable undercurrent of danger and menace.

"I know who you are, Herr Thatcher." Dieter Blick was a nasty piece of work and Max doubted that the two men flanking him in this confined space were the types to go out of their way to help old ladies across the busy road two floors below them. Dieter's English carried a heavy German accent but his vocabulary was excellent; in his business it had to be. "What I would like to know is what you are doing meddling in my business?" At just under six foot he was a good three inches shorter than Max; the thugs either side, however, matched Max's six foot two frame, and from the looks of them wouldn't have looked out of place on an American football team.

"Dieter you've been a naughty boy," Max said with a smile. He hadn't been offered a seat or a cup of anything to drink; this wasn't a social call and both men knew it. Max had had to explain this in rather graphic terms to the 'soldier' who now lying in a crumpled heap downstairs. The thug on the door had been unwilling to allow the former Special Boat Service operative to make his way up to see the man that he had been tracking down for the past four days. Max had put him straight.

Max's company, Falcon Services, had been retained by a Czech company which was becoming increasing fed up with Dieter Blick's business; Blick had been buying product through a chain of 'ghost' companies and then supplying less than angelic organisations with high explosives. It had also become very clear that Dieter was trading in military equipment purloined from various sovereign governments. In short, he was an arms dealer.

"Come now, Herr Thatcher, what gives you the right to stand in my office and make such an allegation?" The man sitting behind his desk was supremely confident that Max was no more than an irritant that could be brushed easily away. His various enterprises had so far avoided being brought into the public gaze despite the efforts of many police forces. He covered his trail very well and if anyone got too close they could be made to simply disappear, permanently. His customers were equally keen to stay off the radar and were only too willing to help with odd favours if it meant they got a little more discount off their next order.

Dieter sat back in his chair and lit a Cuban cigar, and pointedly blew the smoke in Max's direction. "I run a legitimate business."

"Well, I guess if you believe selling munitions to terrorist organisations to be a legitimate business I would have to agree with you." Max stood feet comfortably spread and showed no irritation as the smoke passed him. He liked the odd cigar himself, but didn't miss the obvious intended insult.

"What my customers do with the product is none of my concern, I simply serve a market and if I didn't do it then one of my competitors would be happy to fulfil the orders." Dieter made millions of dollars from his business and his moral values were near the bottom of any scale.

Max bent down and pulled out a large manila file from the small attaché case at his feet. He threw the file unceremoniously on to Dieter's desk. "There's enough information in there to put you away for a long time, Dieter."

"Rubbish, you're bluffing. There has never been anything connecting me directly with any terrorist organisation or illegal activity." Dieter had worked very hard over the years to make sure that nothing ever came back and tainted him directly. It might have been common knowledge in the market that he was a major player but that sort of innuendo didn't stack up in a court of law. He was very happy sitting behind his civil rights when it suited him. As long as he stayed on the right side of his customers they would protect him and as far as the authorities were concerned there was nothing they could do without hard evidence.

Despite himself, and with his curiosity piqued, Dieter couldn't help but pick up the file and started flicking through the material contained therein. He blanched as he scanned the documents; where had this Max Thatcher found all this detail?

Quickly trying to replace the look of shock with a poker face, Dieter decided to go on the front foot. "These are forgeries Herr Thatcher, I've never seen any of these documents and know nothing about the information that you apparently believe links me with these organisations."

Max had seen the man opposite flinch and visibly colour up as he had read the material. Not that any was required, but Max had the confirmation that he sought. His company had been compiling a dossier over several weeks and through their connections across a multitude of intelligence agencies had put together a damning profile on Herr Dieter Blick and his various nefarious enterprises.

"Dieter, that file has now been passed to the Bundesamt für Verfassungsschutz, I sure you're familiar with them."

"Of course I know the BvF," spat Dieter, "what of it? There's nothing here, it's all lies." Max could see that the man was rattled; the arms dealers leisurely puffing on the cigar had now become rather more hurried.

"You're under arrest, Dieter." Max pulled out an official looking document from the smart leather jacket that he was wearing and threw into onto the arms dealer's desk. Switching to German, Dieter snarled instructions to his two thugs. "Jurgen, Kurt, unser freund Thatcher muss uns leider jetzt verlassen. Vielleicht könntet ihr mit ihm eine Hafenfahrt machen. Einfache Fahrt, bitte."

Max spoke better than passable German. "Thanks for the offer of a trip around the harbour, but I really do have other plans."

"Oh but I must insist, Herr Thatcher, take him!" ordered Dieter. The two heavy set men pulled out their concealed weapons and pointed them steadily in Max's direction indicating that he should turn round.

"Goodbye, Herr Thatcher." Dieter didn't like having to do any dirty work himself, but in this instance he didn't believe that he had time to call in a favour. He had to get rid of Max as quickly as possible; the material in the file would have to be dealt with later. He'd put a few calls into his contacts in the police force and make sure some if not all of the information disappeared.

Greg, sitting in the unmarked BfV van across the road from the office, gave a thumbs-up to the other men and a woman in the confined area. "We've got open threat on tape, need to get hold off those files now. Dieter's prints will be all over those bills of lading and that'll do for proof." It wasn't ethical, but then Dieter didn't play by the rules of the game either and a little bit of massaging the evidence seemed a small amount of illegality in the overall scheme of things.

Helga Evers, the head of the BfV, nodded. They couldn't have gone in directly as a Government agency but working alongside Max they had come up with this scheme. There was enough intent on the tape to be able to prosecute Dieter for wishing to do harm to Max and finger prints all over the ships manifestos linked the arms dealer to the trades. "Agreed, let Max know we have enough."

The two thugs pushed Max roughly out of the door to Dieter's office and onwards towards the top of the stairs leading down to the unremarkable street entrance. "We've got what we need, Max," came through in Max's ear piece. Max stopped in his tracks and made to bend down to tie his shoe laces, Kurt the closer of the two gunmen kicked him hard in the backside. This was all the distraction that Max required.

Max made as though he had apparently been knocked off balance and rolled forward, the pair behind him laughed in unison. "Steh auf!" said Kurt. Rather than standing up as instructed, Max completed his roll forward and pulled out in a single motion the pistol that he had strapped to his right ankle. His two guards didn't see what he had done until it was too late as Max from a crouching position fired off a single round into each man. At that range, the SIG 9mm carried a heavy punch and the two 'kill' chest shots knocked his captors onto their backs. Max stood up and kicked the fallen men's guns away from them; they weren't dead but he doubted they would survive.

Max covered the sixty feet back to Dieter's office in a couple of seconds. He kicked the door down and rolled away to the side outside of the office. Dieter had heard the gunshots and was standing behind his desk, as the door had been smashed in he had fired four rounds into the void where he had anticipated Max would be standing.

"Dieter, give it up. It's all over." Max was sitting with his back to the wall next to the open door. He could here Greg and a couple of BvF agents running up the stairs. Dieter's considered response was to fire off another couple of rounds into the wall of his office behind which Max was crouched.

"Fuck you, Max." From where Max was sitting he could hear the road noise suddenly increase. *He's opened the window*, thought Max. He didn't remember there being a fire escape. Was he seriously planning on jumping? *From that height he is most likely going to break a leg*, mused Max.

"Hi Greg, what kept you?" Max had now been joined by the reinforcements.

"Weren't you supposed to get the guys outside so we could take care of them rather than you shooting them in here?" Greg responded cheerfully.

"Possibly," Max said with a grin, "but I didn't want to give our boy in there," he pointed over his shoulder into Dieter's office, "a chance to work out that shredding the documents might be a good idea."

Dieter fired off a couple of more shots in the general direction of the people outside of the office. He was a desperate man.

Greg indicated for the BvF agents to stay behind him; he could see that one of the men that Max had shot looked dead whilst the other was receiving some immediate treatment from a paramedic that had been called in. "What do you want to do, Max?"

"Well, much as I would like to put a bullet in the guy, I suspect Helga would like him alive as he must be able to provide us with a lot of information about the terrorist groups that he has been supplying." Max considered their options. "Got a stun grenade?" Greg nodded.

"Helga, are you there?" Max knew that she was listening to his every word via the wiretap that he had been wearing.

"Yes Max. And yes we would like him alive please!" came the response in his ear piece. "Make sure you cover the street, I reckon Dieter might be considering jumping."

"Got it covered," responded the senior BvF officer.

"OK, we're going to lob in a couple of stun grenades and see if that slows him down." Max looked across at Greg. "Ready?"

Greg pulled out two grenades and pitched one across to Max. "Yep, on three?" Max nodded and pulled the pin whilst still holding down the release mechanism.

The men looked across at one another and nodded in unison as they rolled the grenades into the room. The explosions were deafening. Before the sound had finished reverberating around Dieter's office, Max and Greg in turn dived through the open door.

Dieter was curled up in a foetal position next to his desk; they could see blood running down the side of his face from his shattered eardrums. He had dropped his weapon. Max needed no second bidding and quickly covered the distance between him and the prone man. He kicked away the pistol as he took his position standing over Dieter with his gun pointed steadily at the arms dealer's head.

"Well, Dieter, it looks like you've got a bit of explaining to do to your friends at the BvF." The damage to his hearing would heal in time; for now he couldn't hear a word that Max had said, but his look of rage and pure hatred told Max that Herr Bick was less than happy with the outcome of that morning's meeting.

Christ's Hospital, West Sussex - Monday Morning, 07.18

"Morning Helen, how comes the train has been cancelled again?" asked a highly agitated David Smith. Despite the ambient temperature being near freezing, he felt hot and bothered; he was hung over. Sunday had been one long extended drinking session with a couple of his soccer pals down at the local pub and he had failed to get up for the earlier train as he had originally intended. He was supposed to be at a meeting in London's West End by nine am and, from the looks of things, what had already been a tight timetable was going to become totally unworkable.

The petite uniformed woman sitting behind the Perspex screen checked he computer. "Looks like the 07.20 Victoria train has broken down around Barnham and you'll be best off catching the 07.40 London Bridge train and changing at East Croydon," came the friendly courteous reply to David's question. Helen had seen it all happen before so many times and the regular commuters knew that she was really on 'their side' and, for the most part, they shared in good humour her frustration with continually having to pass on the 'happy news' of cancellations and delays.

David stuck his head out of the ticket office and looked at the electronic sign; apparently the London Bridge train was now running late. "I guess the London Bridge train has got stuck behind the broken down one," he said to a couple of his fellow commuters who were milling around aimlessly in the cold, dark and damp January morning. "Looks like it," agreed a middle aged woman wrapped up in a ski jacket. David recognised her from seeing her on the platform many times before but didn't know her name.

"Train's going to be a zoo, two train loads packed into a single service," was his parting comment as he pulled his overcoat tight and made his way along the southbound platform and down through the subway which brought him out onto Platform Two. The woman followed in his wake; they looked almost like a couple, but neither knew the other's name nor would dare ask and break the unspoken taboo of communicating with fellow passengers uninvited.

The 07.40 London Bridge train was now, according to the apologetic periodical announcements, scheduled to arrive at 08.15. This had a predictable result: rather than two train loads of commuters boarding, this meant that three sets squeezed their way on to the 07.55 Victoria service. Understandably, no one was really sure that the London Bridge service was ever going to arrive so no one was prepared to take the chance and wait.

Even this far out from Central London, some 45 miles, these three trains were normally pretty full in their own right. Combining three trains in such short order had the predictable effect of filling the twelve-carriage train almost to capacity even before it reached later stops where larger numbers of commuters would typically board.

By the time the 07.55 Southern service, which had started out from Bognor Regis, reached Clapham Junction it was standing room only. The somewhat belated offer of "de-classing" first class accommodation so that anyone could stand there, without fear of criminal prosecution for not having the requisite tickets did little to improve the mood of the silently fuming, hard-pressed commuting British public. To many who had to suffer the daily routine, it was unfathomable how rail fares continued to relentlessly increase. Service levels did not appear to markedly improve and the passenger volumes increased without any additional rolling stock being added. Many assumed that the politicians sitting in their Government chauffeur-driven limos had little real exposure to the realities of being a commuter.

Frankly, most hard pressed commuters thought it was a disgrace how people were regularly crammed into carriages designed to accommodate half their number and that Monday morning, with an unwelcome cancellation and subsequent knock-on effect, the problems were compounded.

Despite this, one could hear only the noise of the train or the slightly too loud personal hifi; speaking on the trains at rush hour was strictly *verboten* - an unwritten rule that almost all regular commuters seemingly followed without complaint. Tourists or inexperienced travellers could be picked out easily; they would be the ones talking. One could sit next to the same person for years, and many people do, without sharing a single conversation.

~

An unkempt Jeremiah was standing on the platform at Clapham Junction with Jana, a good looking long-legged blonde of Polish stock, as the delayed train pulled in. He Snapchatted the six digit number on the front of the train to Gabriella, some three miles to his north, and handed Jana the large rucksack.

"Make sure you don't let this out of your sight, Jana – they're some really important books in here," he tapped the bag, "and Gabriella will be really upset if she doesn't have them for the shop this morning."

"I got it, no problem." Jana swung the bag onto her back. "How many books are there in here? It weighs a ton!"

She had been working part time for a cousin of hers in a cafe near Battersea for the past couple of months when she'd been introduced to Jeremiah one evening at a local pub. They'd had a few drinks and got on pretty well, eventually ending up in a ropey old flat on the south side of the river near Wandsworth Bridge.

Her original plan was to come to the UK for a few months, maybe a year; improve her English and make some money before returning to her native Poland. Work had been harder to find than planned and frankly she was no better off in London than she had been at home; so much for the streets being paved with gold. The offer that morning of helping Jeremiah out at short notice and making £50 cash in hand for her troubles was not an offer that she could afford to turn down.

"I've no idea," said Jeremiah with a grin as he helped adjust the straps to spread the load more comfortably. "Anyway, you won't have to carry them for long," he added. Apparently, or so he had explained to Jana, he had other errands to run that morning.

The twelve-carriage green and white liveried train slowed and came to a stop on Platform twelve. The pair were standing near the front but they could see from the couple of carriages that had already passed that it was full to bursting point. "Why don't we wait for the next one, Jeremiah? This one looks terribly full."

"You'll be fine," he said encouragingly as the doors opened and a couple of passengers stepped onto the platform to allow those who were really getting off there to disembark. It's doubtful that, had she not been such a good looking young woman, any space would have been found for her lithe body and rather incongruous travelling rucksack. The doors closed and Jeremiah waved as his 'girlfriend' managed to give a big smile in return whilst, with the willing help of a couple of students, she dropped her luggage onto the floor of the carriage.

Less than five minutes later the train was moving slowly through the last station before Victoria, situated in the shadow of the Battersea Power Station and overlooking the dogs' home sharing the same name. Gabriella, from her vantage point on the north side of the river, could see the train approaching and with the help of her high powered binoculars checked the six numbers showing on the front carriage. Satisfied they matched the numbers that Jeremiah had just sent through, she pulled the small transceiver from the heavy parka coat that she was wearing to keep out the January cold.

"Ladies and gentleman, this is the conductor." The train began edging its way across Victoria railway bridge. "On behalf of Southern Rail, I should like to apologise for the late running of this service and the overcrowding which has resulted due to the broken down train in the Arun Valley this morning."

"I bet he should," mouthed David under his breath to no one in particular. The hangover was beginning to kick in with a vengeance and he was in desperate need of a coffee or something stronger. He checked his watch. Bollocks, he was going to be at least twenty minutes late, an important meeting too. *Good fun yesterday but shouldn't have shared that last bottle of red wine when I got home*, he mused.

The train picked up a bit of pace as if it could cover the last half a mile in record time to make up for the delays experienced. Midway across the open water, Gabriella pushed the button.

The third carriage on the 06.13 from Bognor Regis originally destined for London Victoria buckled as the Semtex explosives, surrounded in nails, detonated in a huge ball of flame and destruction. Lethal shrapnel flew the length of the carriage killing half the occupants instantly. Jana's well-proportioned five foot ten inches of body, admired earlier, was vapourised in an instant in the intense heat of the explosion. There would be nothing left of her to identify, nor the people that she had been standing cheek by jowl with, 'guarding' her bag.

The occupants of the neighbouring carriages were covered in pieces of flying metal and body parts. For those not killed outright or badly injured, this was the least of their problems as the carriages twisted into the air and moved inexorably towards the edge of the bridge. The lead carriage, now on its side, couldn't help but slide through the restraining wall and down into the muddy Thames that was flowing at high water, dragging with it the rest of the carriages.

It would take several days to establish just how many people were killed in the initial blast compared with the number that was drowned, as eight of the over-filled carriages ended up making an unwelcome tourist attraction just outside of one of the greatest cities in the world.

Chiswick, West London – Monday, Mid-Morning

"Morning Pete. Good weekend?" Max, dressed in jeans, his favourite leather boots and heavy duty rugby shirt, wandered into the open plan offices of Falcon Services feeling a little jaded. He'd been to watch some rugby on the Sunday with a few friends in Richmond and was feeling a little fragile. *Probably well deserved,* he thought after having worked his way through double figures on the pint count and, from what he could remember, a half decent curry.

Max kept up a strict training regime, something which had been drilled in to him during his time in the Special Boat Service. He liked the odd drink and since the terrible loss of Clare had for the most part had kept a pretty low social profile. Yesterday had been something of break in his otherwise pretty dour existence, his daily focus being almost exclusively his work.

"Hi, Max. Yeah, good thanks. At least I wasn't on that train this morning. Terrible business." Peter Owens had worked for the firm for a couple of years. His role was focused mainly in the information-gathering arena as opposed to being out in the field. Max had listened to the car radio on the way in and predictably there had been nothing on but various reports from the scene of the carnage. He'd flicked through the various stations but none could shed any light on exactly what had happened though, from eye reports, it was pretty clear to Max that a large explosive device of some description had been employed. He idly wondered whether Herr Dieter Blick, now hopefully to become a long term guest of the German penal system, had been in some way responsible for providing the munitions for the outrage.

"Some sick bastards out there, Pete," observed Max; he knew this as truism from his own experiences. "Is Patrick in?" he asked as he made his way across the open plan space, acknowledging other members of the team as he went.

"Yes, he's been in for hours and is in his office - sorry, your office," confirmed the investigator. Many people in the office were still coming to terms with the new arrangements.

"No problem, you were right the first time." Max replied cheerfully as he made his way across the office towards his 'old' residence. Since his recent mission involving the De Heerden brothers a couple of months earlier, Max had taken much more of a back seat in the running of the business and handed day-to-day control to Patrick. The loss of Clare still burned deeply within him and he was far happier being out in the field working on active projects, rather than having time to think over what might have been.

The office door was half open. He knocked and simultaneously walked into the room. Patrick was on the phone speaking French to one of his contacts. The acting CEO looked up from his call and gave Max a small wave indicating that he would be finished shortly. Max sat in a comfortable chair opposite and waited patiently for the call to come to its natural conclusion. He was in no particular hurry; he'd finished up the work in Germany and was keen to see what he could get involved with next.

"Bien sûr, oui." Max tuned in to the call; his French was pretty good. He prided himself on being able to converse in most European languages, a courtesy as much as anything as most of his counterparts spoke far better English than he could their native languages. He translated Patrick's end of the conversation.

"Gerard, I'll start taking a look through the files here. Nothing springs to mind immediately but, of course, anything we have is yours." Max couldn't hear the other end of the call but whatever was being discussed was clearly pretty heavy as Patrick's demeanour was anything but relaxed.

There was a pause whilst Gerard was clearly passing on some requests. "That's a good idea. Look it's just coming up to ten amhere. Why don't we plan on another call around midday my time. Does that work for you?"

Obviously it did from the other end. "Bon, au revoir." Patrick put the phone down and looked across at his old friend and the owner of Falcon Services. "That was Gerard Faure in Paris, not a happy bunny."

"Is he still working for the DRM? I thought he might have retired by now." Over the years Max had had several dealings with the Direction du Renseignement Militaire, loosely translated as the military secret police.

"Yes, very much so. He's the top guy now," confirmed Patrick.

"What's got him all excited? Have we got a team stepping on his toes or something?" Max was a little confused as to why Patrick would be on a call with the head of the DRM; bit off their beaten path as a rule. And as far as he was aware they didn't have any projects currently running in France.

"No, he's looking for information," responded Patrick. "Late night, Max?" He spotted at once that Max was looking a little jaded.

"A little, I'm going to get a cup of tea. Then you can tell me all about Gerard. Can I get you something?" Max pulled himself out of the chair.

"Black coffee, please," Patrick said, following him out of the room as he made his way to the kitchen area.

Boston - Monday, 06.20

The weather in the New England area had been remarkably temperate for the time of year; it was comfortably above freezing even though there was an uncluttered sky and the moon could be seen clearly. The Monday morning rush hour was just getting under way in earnest, and the wide freeways leading into the centre of town would be clogged within the hour.

Out on open water, Gary powered up the type 91 SAM-2 Surface to Air missile launcher, a must in every delusional terrorist's armoury. Acquiring one had been remarkably easy if one knew where to look; he'd started with the Internet and had gone from there. He was dressed in his favourite hunting garb, camouflage jacket and woolly hat to keep him safe from any morning chill. He was standing alone on the aft deck of an old wooden lobster fishing boat that he was currently in the process of re-conditioning. In the half-light he would have been hard to spot from any further than fifty yards away and at that time of the morning the Atlantis Marina was basically deserted, so he had little concern for the prospect of being interrupted.

To his south, less than a half a mile from where he stood, he could see the end of one of the main runways at Logan International Airport jutting out into the bay. He checked his watch, the luminescent dial reading 06.30: the appointed hour. It had been decided that this was a good time to target a commuter flight making the relatively short hop down to New York or Washington.

To be blunt, Gary had little concern for which airplane he took out; the only thing as far as he was concerned was to select one of the imperialist US airlines. At 06.32 Delta 367 lumbered down runway 4R/22L packed with half-asleep passengers recovering from their weekend exploits and looking forward to catching up with some lost sleep on their short trip south. Many of the passengers made this same trip every day, using the flight as an alternative to living in the conurbations of New York or Washington. The stunning countryside around the Boston area more than made up for the inconvenience and associated expense of the flight.

The Boeing 737-800 rose slowly into the air, with her payload of 150 passengers and eight crew all apparently safely secured in their seats. The instructions contained in the box had been remarkably straightforward and easy to digest, not much to it apart from point and shoot. Gary spread his feet and lined up the laser sight with the aircraft as it made its way towards him. Satisfied that he had his target locked, he released the SAM. The radical, in his late twenties, watched with a mixture of awe and sick fascination as the missile briefly lit up the marina and covered the distance to the commercial airliner in a handful of seconds. To his warped mind, as the missile snaked off, it looked just like something out of one of the violent video games that he so enjoyed playing.

The missile found its target, striking in the middle of the soft underbelly of the jet where the wings joined the fuselage. The SAM's high explosives lit up the early morning sky in the general area of the marina; Gary was suitably impressed. This was only a foretaste of what was to come as the following explosion, caused by the fully-loaded high octane aviation fuel tanks in the wings combusting, threw a red blanket of light across the whole bay and Boston suburbs. The sound was deafening and cut through the dull morning hum of the Boston commuting traffic making its way in the distance along the shore of the bay. Then just as quickly there was, by contrast, almost a total silence as the plane made the short descent into the bay. Gary had watched as the starboard wing had separated from the main fuselage, which itself could then be seen to be disintegrating as it lost its structural integrity. Flight 367 broke apart and made its way in pieces to crash into the bay in a series of impressive splashes.

Gary, more than satisfied with his morning's work, returned to the boat's small bridge area and put the engine into gear. He made no effort to look for survivors as he sailed slowly out of the bay. He decided that he would let the early morning news channels spread the word rather than risking a call or sending a text to Control.

Chiswick – Monday, Late Morning

Max and Patrick were continuing their discussion about Patrick's earlier call with Gerard Faure, head of the DRM in Paris.

"What information is he looking for?" queried Max.

"Well, I doubt you'll know about this yet but there's been a bomb let off in the Paris Metro, apparently the device went off at nine thirty their time this morning," explained Patrick.

"Are you kidding?! Jesus." Max was shocked.

"All our UK news feeds have been concentrating on the Victoria explosion so it's not made it into the public domain yet. The French police are publicly putting it down to a gas explosion, but Gerard has it on good authority that it wasn't an accident. Apparently a lot of people have been killed and looks like whatever was let off was covered in nails."

Max stretched out his six foot two frame. "Ummm, doesn't sound like a gas explosion does it?"

Details hadn't been released to the media in London about the nail element to the device detonated on the packed commuter train – Patrick, though, through his contacts, already had the lowdown on this.

"Max, you need to know that the bomb in London was also wrapped in nails."

"That's more than coincidence," stated Max.

"I agree. There seem to be other similarities and I imagine that's why Gerard was coming on to us, to see if we knew any more than what London was telling our friends in Paris." During their years of active service and now also in semi-civilian life, Max and his team members had built contacts across the globe within every sovereign national secret service. Falcon Services was a known 'contractor' and recognised as a good source of information for the 'good guys'. Their reputation for absolute discretion and trustworthiness was unblemished, something of which Max was duly proud.

"What else do we know about London?" asked Max. The fact that whoever had done this terrible thing had made it that much worse, if that were possible, by lacing the device with nails beggared belief. He wasn't surprised that there were more details known to Patrick than he had heard about on the radio. There had been a steady stream of updates that he had listened to whilst he had made the short drive from his home, a barge moored on the Thames, to the office.

"Current thinking is that high explosives were detonated in the third carriage. Can't be sure yet but from the damage caused and the heat signature it looks like it was Semtex. The damage is horrific and the guys on the scene have found the carriages laced with nails. Max, the bomb was dirty, designed to kill and maim as many as possible. It also looks like it was detonated remotely."

"How so?" asked Max.

Patrick explained the origin of the train's fateful journey and how it had been delayed. "The bomb definitely went off inside the carriage and not externally. The force of the impact threw the carriage off the rails and took the rest of the train with it over the edge into the river with its momentum. To get the most effect you'd have wanted to blow it up on the bridge, and because of the delay it couldn't have been timed, so it's logical someone was waiting for it to cross. If it wasn't a suicide bomber then whoever did this watched it come out of Battersea and then pushed the button would be my guess."

Max considered this for a moment. "On the face of it sounds like there are several similarities with the bomb in Paris but I can't recall of there ever being a simultaneously executed in both capitals." He paused for a moment. "The one on the Metro was let off underground, right?"

Patrick referred to his notes. "Yes, went off between the stop for the Louvre and Pont Neuf. I can only imagine that it would have made a hell of a mess in such a confined space. Christ, what sort of a sick bastard would want to pull off these types of atrocities?"

Before Max had a chance to comment further there was a knock on the office door.

Patrick looked past Max towards the door. "Hi Pete, what's up?"

"Guys, you should come and see this. It's all over the news. Someone has just shot down an airliner in Boston!"

Downing Street – Monday, Lunchtime

What had started as a terrible morning had, despite all reasonable expectations, incredibly become even worse.

"I've just got off the phone with the President. He's put the US on DEFCON 3." The British Prime Minister's two visitors sitting in his private office that morning knew that this was two levels off the highest security alert, DEFCON 1 being the highest, indicating that war was imminent.

Rupert Taylor, who had only been in office for a few months, checked his watch. "What time are we meeting the rest of the team?" He had taken over from his predecessor who had been murdered in the De Heerdens' orchestrated bombings and was still learning the ropes of being the leader of the Country.

"Twenty minutes, Prime Minister," replied Admiral Walker. The chair of the Joint Chiefs of Staff was a resource that Rupert relied upon immensely to provide guidance and insight. The PM recognised that he was personally highly inexperienced in these types of situations and was big enough to acknowledge his shortcomings.

"Jessica," the PM turned his attention to the head of MI6, "What do we know so far about the bombing at Victoria?" He had read the initial reports; the casualty figure was going to be horrendous, and he knew that he had to make a public statement sooner rather than later to return confidence to the millions of very frightened commuters across the UK.

Technically an incident of this nature would fall to MI5 as it was domestic, but he had called in MI6 in the absence of Charlie Marsh, the head of MI5, who was due to arrive within the hour. In the interim Rupert was keen to try and get up to speed as much as possible; in any event he had little truck with the dividing lines between MI5 and MI6. He appreciated the logic, purely from the standpoint of focus, for one organisation to be responsible for internal security whilst the other for more international matters. In truth it looked like the problems of today looked as they were far broader than simply those all too clearly present in the UK.

Jessica Brown, dressed as usual in a smart dark business suit, took a quick look at the file open in front of her and began to give her report. In her role as head of MI6 she was responsible for overseas matters of National Security but unlike some of her predecessors she had worked hard to build a good relationship with her counterpart in MI5. As a result there was now generally a very good flow of information between the organisations, something which had not always been the case.

"From what both Charlie and I have been able to work out, the London bombing was much as you would have heard or seen on the television. What we haven't released is that the bomb detonated was a massive nail bomb, particularly nasty. Looks in principle a similar sort of modus operandi to the one that went off in Paris."

"We've been able to match the bomb types already?" asked the PM.

"No Sir. I meant more from the type of engagement. In neither case was there any warning. Both devices were aimed at busy commuter trains and both involved nails bombs. This wasn't simply about killing as many people as possible, it was also about the attacks being carried out in the most vicious way possible." Jessica paused for breath "Really nasty pieces of work behind this. As far as the US business is concerned we only have very sketchy information but it looks like the plane was brought down with a missile, clearly portable. Again, no warnings. No obvious connection, apart for the timings, to what happened here or in Paris; but it does seem more than coincidental."

The Admiral had been reading through some of the printed briefing material. "Has anybody put their hand up yet to claim responsibility?"

"No Sir." In a less formal environment the head of MI6 might have called him by his first name, Gordon, but that felt out of place sitting in the PM's private office. Ever since the pair had worked together in a slightly unofficial way to help resolve the issue with the De Heerden brothers, they had become firm friends. Jessica was always careful not to overstep the mark in public, though, and therefore always maintained the formality expected.

"What do you think we ought to do, Gordon?" probed the Prime Minister. As PM he believed he'd earned the right to use first names and he was keen to assert his authority, not to be seen as playing second fiddle.

The Admiral rubbed his haggard features with both hands, *I'm getting too old for this shit*, he thought privately. "Let's see what Charlie can bring to the table. We have to make some public statements about what has happened this morning in London. At the same time, PM, we clearly should go to great lengths to extend our condolences and expressions of horror for the Paris and Boston atrocities." He paused for a moment and looked earnestly at Rupert. "The most important thing is that we don't appear rattled, and that we do everything that we can to convey full confidence that we are on top of the situation."

"Agreed, but we have nothing to go on or work with." Rupert Taylor hadn't expected to be in this position when he had gone into politics. As a career politician, he had always hoped to become PM and to one day get the top job. His recent enforced rapid promotion to the highest office had obviously been a shock not only to him but also to the country as a whole. Inheriting the role through the predecessor's assassination had not been expected; he had lost a good friend as well as a great Leader in his opinion. He was an unknown, untried quantity to many people in government circles and even less well known to the general population. A politician that had operated somewhat in the shadows had now been thrown almost totally unprepared into the full glare of the media spotlight. Leading a nation in a time of crisis was always in some way a perverse boyhood dream, but now that he was actually in that role he felt lost.

The PM privately mused that pitching election manifestos, from various soapboxes, that may or may not ever come to anything tangible was one thing. Standing in front of the world and being judged on how he was handling this type of situation was of a completely different order.

Admiral Walker was neither blind nor insensitive to the emotions that were clearly running through the man sitting opposite him. He recognised that men under live fire for the first time reacted in different ways. These next few days would be the making or breaking of the Prime Minister.

"Prime Minister, you'll be fine. You've got a good team around you and we will get the bastards who did this." His tone and demeanour left little room for doubt or indecision in the minds of Jessica and Rupert. Admiral Walker was a leader of men, a hard earned right and he carried the less experienced and the insecure with him through sheer force of personality and outwardly calm presence.

Privately he was very worried about the nature of the disconnected yet clearly interrelated events and he was worried that there would be more to follow; a premonition that within a few short hours was to be proved correct.

Amsterdam – Monday, Early Afternoon

Control took a look at the cheap watch that she always chose to wear when not in the public gaze. 14.09 blinked the LCD display. Another twenty minutes or so before the next piece of the puzzle would fall into place; so far everything had gone according to plan. *Well, why wouldn't it*, she mused; she had spent a year in the development of this great game and she had gone through every element of the model in her devious mind. The apparent randomness of her strikes would destabilize everyone and give them nothing to work with, nothing to connect the atrocities back to her.

She was sitting naked and cross-legged on her large double bed at the top of the old town house that she had bought in the centre of Amsterdam's world famous red light district. In her view it was hardly notorious any more, it had become over the years even more of a tourist trap and had somewhat lost its 'edginess'. The Dutch Government had been loath to completely kill it off and continued to allow tourists from around the world to come to the City, built over the myriad of canals, to enjoy a smoke of this or that, safe in the knowledge that they weren't going to get prosecuted for smoking drugs in public as they would in their native homelands.

One could still buy hard drugs on a street corner if one were stupid enough to trust a complete stranger not to sell you a small plastic bag of talc or some such nonsense. The windows overlooking the canals in the centre of the red light district still had their titillating displays on show for all, and blow jobs could be exchanged for a few euros in any number of bars and pubs around the centre of town. It seemed highly incongruous to her that one could buy drugs legally and then not being able to smoke a cigarette in many of the bars because of the comparatively new anti-smoking rules.

With this thought still on her mind, she flipped open a packet of Marlboro Reds and lit up her umpteenth cigarette of the day. She had invested heavily in a number of silent smoke extractors to ensure that the house and its contents didn't smell of smoke. An odour, ironically, that she didn't particularly enjoy - but she reasoned that the nicotine fix was better than getting hooked on the stronger stuff. She was something of a control freak. No, she mused that if she were totally honest she was a complete control freak and always wanted to be in charge of her faculties.

The three television sets dotted around her bedroom, all set to silent, were displaying the results of her planning against the backdrop of some music playing though her very expensive sound system. She inhaled the cigarette smoke deeply and idly played with her intimate parts with her free hand. Watching all the death and destruction that she had wrought was turning her on. She stubbed the cigarette out and rolled over so that she could reach into one of the bedside cabinets and pulled out a favourite sex toy of hers.

She lay on her back and pinched her nipples in turn with her left hand until they had become hard. With her right hand the played expertly with her vibrator on the outer folds of her vagina before concentrating on the 'secret' muscle at the top her now very wet opening. Splaying her legs, she arched her back and drove the humming and pulsating machine deep within her. Closing her eyes to increase the stimulus, she imagined in her mind that she was sharing the experience with a man and a woman. She liked threesomes.

From the corner of her eye she saw the news that she had been eagerly expecting and this took her over the edge so that she climaxed in time with the new outrage now being shown live on TV across the globe.

San Francisco – Monday, 05.30

Asad pulled the sixteen-litre Mack Titan 605hp beast of a truck across to the side of the freeway and turned on the hazard warning lights. He was well aware that he wouldn't have long, as the traffic police stationed on the south end of the bridge would be notified about the 'broken down' truck almost immediately. He jumped out of the truck's cab and went back 40 feet to the end of the first trailer of two that he had driven up from Monterey Bay that morning.

Satisfied that all was as it was supposed to be, he flicked the switch on the package strapped to the base of the lead trailer. The digital counter indicated 180 seconds. He watched the counter go down to 150 before he turned his back on the huge mobile bomb and crossed the short distance to the railings overlooking the city of San Francisco. In the middle distance he could see the island of Alcatraz with its prison perched on the crest of the small hill at the centre of the outcrop of rock. The former prison was still lit up for the tourists even this early in the morning.

In the far distance it was hard to make out the individual buildings that made up the San Francisco skyline. He liked San Francisco as a city and had visited it many times to enjoy the different delights that were on offer. Asad and his brother had been living in America for the last five years; they had worked hard and built a successful software business. Despite having the financial capacity to support his family members still stuck in his homeland, they had not been allowed to come to America and escape their war-torn homeland. When they had been killed by a suicide bomber something had flipped in his mind and that of his younger brother. They held the western powers responsible for the death of their kin; it was all political and about oil. The Americans spoke of freedom and yet did nothing to help the oppressed unless there was commercial gain to be had.

What he was about to do was a statement against the USA's foreign policy and he was pleased that his actions would go down in history. He hoped that the individual loss of life as a direct consequence would be kept at a minimum. Hopefully, people would understand that it could have been that much worse had he driven his truck and attached trailers down on to the packed waterfront area of the city.

The traffic on the iconic landmark at that time of the morning was very light and he could see the flashing blue lights of a speeding police car making its way uninterrupted to the midpoint of the suspension bridge. It wouldn't take them long to cover the three quarters of a mile, but he knew it was long enough to serve his purpose.

Not exactly sure which way was due east, he pointed himself in the direction of the city of Mecca and made his peace with his god.

The police car was still some 400 yards away when the comparatively small bomb on the side of the truck's lead trailer exploded and thereby detonated the massive 4000lb fertiliser bomb contained within. As intended, the first major explosion set off the second trailer containing a similar amount of explosive material. The effect was cataclysmic and the shock waves blew a couple of passing cars over as though they were feathers caught in a gale force wind.

The explosives in both containers had been rigged, as far as possible, to ensure that most of the force was driven downwards. However, in order to make sure of the desired results the bombers had simply gone for volume of explosive material. Where the truck with its two accompanying trailers had once stood, there was now a gaping hole in the bridge; the void became an elongated crack which rapidly spread across both carriages of the freeway. The entire six lane road buckled and twisted under the weight of the enormous explosions so that the supporting wires pulled themselves free. Without the thick steel cables to carry the colossal weight, the entire expanse of freeway only had one way to go: straight down.

Where once there was a mile span of freeway, there was now only a massive chasm across the San Francisco Bay, framed by the two red iconic towers that had once supported the Golden Gate Bridge.

Downing Street, London – Early Afternoon

"I simply don't believe it, you can't be serious? You're telling me that someone has driven a truck onto the Golden Gate Bridge and blown it up!?" Rupert Taylor's senses were frazzled: a bomb in London, one on the Paris Metro and two terrorist attacks on the US mainland. "What the fuck is going on?"

Admiral Walker sat dispassionately on the British Prime Minister's right hand side; his mind was reeling too, but he knew better than to show his emotions too openly. In times of crisis, one had to at least create the impression of calmness or all around would start losing their heads and begin to panic. He could see that the PM was, understandably, struggling to cope with an array of disasters of these magnitudes unfolding in such a short space of time.

The COBRA meeting had been in session for a couple of hours prior to the news of the latest outrage on the west coast of the States becoming known. The Cabinet Office Briefing Room 'A', shortened to COBRA, was packed with the heads of the armed forces, both heads of MI5 and MI6 were present and there was a number of department heads and cabinet members. The PM's outburst met with silence, for no one in the room in truth had any idea what was going on.

Both Jessica Brown and Charlie Marsh, the MI6 and MI5 heads respectively, had given their reports. In short, they didn't know an awful lot more than they had a couple of hours earlier. Forensics on the train had been hampered because the Thames was swollen from winter rains and the tide had yet to ebb fully. Heavy lifting equipment had been brought in, but only a couple of the badly deformed coaches had been recovered from their watery resting points.

"What have we done to try and find out who placed the London bomb?" asked Admiral Walker, keen to get the meeting back on track. From his perspective, the imperative now was to work on trying to find out what on earth was going on and who was behind these terrible atrocities.

"We've been checking all the closed circuit TV that we have to see if anything useful comes up," offered Charlie Marsh, the head of MI5. "From what we know, the bomb must have been physically pretty large."

"Presumably it's a bit like looking for the proverbial needle?" commented Karen Bell, one of the permanent under-secretaries in the room. "How do you know when the bomb was put on board? For all we know the package could have been placed where we had no CCTV coverage."

"You're right of course, Karen, but we have to start somewhere." Charlie couldn't fault her logic, but had nothing else to offer at this juncture.

"How about the onboard cameras?" queried the PM. He was well aware that in order to stamp out anti-social behaviour and provide a degree of security for train staff and passengers alike there were now, on most trains, recorder CCTVs in operation. He couldn't help think it of minimal comfort that at every railway station, both over ground and on the tube network, as well as on every train, announcements were made continually asking passengers not to leave packages unattended for fear of them being removed by security services and possibly being damaged or destroyed. It was a hopeless task to try and police all the public areas in the UK. He acknowledged that realistically, without implementing security procedures such as the ones in use at the airports, how could one check for bombs or weapons? The likelihood of these types of measures being introduced across the board was negligible; it simply wasn't practical.

"We've recovered the CCTV disk and are taking a look," confirmed the head of MI5, "but from initial reports I understand that the train was so full it's hard to see much of anything."

"Do we know anything about the device itself?" enquired the Admiral.

Charlie looked over at the Admiral. "Forensics are saying military grade high explosives, logically we've established the bomb was most likely detonated remotely or by the person carrying it. The timings and delay of the train suggest that a timed detonation appears unlikely," replied Charlie.

"How the hell did these people get hold of military explosives?" The PM was staggered it was possible for people to acquire this type of bomb-making material and his tone had reflected this.

"All too easy I'm afraid, Sir. There's a big black market out there for weapons and if you're prepared to pay the money you can get hold of pretty well anything." The head of MI5 almost shrugged his shoulders in resignation as he delivered the answer.

"So where do we go from here?" Rupert was getting frustrated with the lack of progress or any tangible information with which to work.

"We've got people out all over the place looking for information, Sir. Something will turn up," offered Charlie. He rather wished that he'd kept quiet; it was a weak answer and he knew it.

The PM almost exploded with pent up frustration. "Frankly it's not good enough. You guys in the secret services and police are supposed to stop this sort of thing happening in the first instance and from ..."

Admiral Walker saw little profit in letting Rupert have a rant so cut across the PM. "Prime Minister, everyone in this room shares a common set of goals. I am certain that we will have plenty of time later to consider what we might have done differently. For now we need to focus on the who, and probably the why, so that we can stop it happening again. What concerns me is that there has been no admission of responsibility. The fact that there were no warnings, of any description, given. That all the targets were entirely civilian combined with the brutality of the attacks makes me believe we are dealing with some very unpleasant characters."

The Admiral paused for breath and took his time looking around the room before continuing. "This atrocity was an attack on our civilian population. It was clearly designed to kill indiscriminately as many people as possible. The fact that they picked a packed commuter train suggests that they are trying to undermine the fabric of society. How many people are going to want to come to work tomorrow?"

With no response encouraged and none forthcoming he pressed on. "Ladies and gentleman, I believe all the events of today are somehow linked. I do not believe it a coincidence that three sovereign nations have been attacked all within the space of a few short hours. Your job is to find out who is the ring leader who has coordinated these terrible events." There were nods of assent from all round the table. Rupert Taylor rather wished that it were him making the statement but understood that he had begun to try to play a blame game rather than trying to fix the problems that they all faced. Another lesson learned, the PM committed to himself that he would try and be more statesmanlike in future.

"With your agreement, Prime Minister, I would suggest that we should reconvene in four hours and see what more has been learned?" The Admiral was keen not to be seen to be taking complete control.

"Good idea, Gordon," confirmed the PM.

The meetings attendees began to collate their respective piles of papers and made ready to make their way out of the room.

"Prime Minister, Jessica and Charlie. Please, do you think I might have a moment?" Admiral Walker had another item on his agenda.

The four of them remained seated and waited patiently for the rest of the room to clear.

"What's on your mind, Gordon?" asked Rupert.

"With the agreement of you all, I'm going to suggest that we bring Max Thatcher and his team in to help us on this crisis." This was a something of a bombshell for the heads of MI5 and MI6; if the Prime Minister was surprised, he didn't show it. He knew of Max and his guys and everything was frankly in such a muddle that he thought that he would wait and see what everyone else said before he took any position.

"Admiral, we're more than capable of dealing with the situation. Why would we need an external nongovernmental agency involved?" The head of MI5 saw the suggestion as a direct slur on his organisation's ability to get to the bottom of the current crisis.

Jessica on the other hand could see some logic to the suggestion and was keen to draw out what was behind the Admiral's thought processes. "What do you have in mind, Admiral? You know that between Charlie's and my organisations we've got a couple of hundred operatives out kicking doors and reviewing information."

The Prime Minister was feeling a bit lost. He knew very little about Max and Falcon Services other than by reputation. His tacit agreement to resolving the De Heerden situation had been one of very much arm's length, not wanting to know the details and thereby maintaining full deniability. Admiral Walker was clearly not going to give him that easy option again.

"Please understand that I am not casting aspersions on our teams here in the UK or overseas, but we must face facts. We had no prior warning of any of these events; for all the effort we put into counter terrorism on this occasion, we have failed and failed badly." said the Admiral, not in an aggressive or finger-pointing tone.

Charlie looked across the table at the Admiral and gave a small nod so as to acknowledge the point. He'd known Gordon Walker for a long time and knew that the man wasn't interested in points scoring. "Go on, I'm listening." His initial outburst, he now realised, might easily have been perceived as somewhat parochial and he was keen to be seen not to be blinkered in his approach. He also recognised that, so far, MI5 really hadn't come up with anything terribly useful.

"Here's my logic. Please allow me take you through my thought processes and then obviously we can discuss. Firstly, if we are dealing with a totally unknown quantity - which, as we had no inkling of what we've witnessed today may be a distinct possibility - we have to consider the scenario that it may be that our resources, albeit for the right reasons, are in fact looking in the wrong places. I believe it wouldn't hurt our cause to have someone with a fresh pair of eyes look at what's transpired and see whether they come up with a different picture." The Admiral paused for breath.

"And secondly?" The PM wanted to see the second shoe drop before committing one way or the other.

"I believe it would help our cause having a group acting without the restraints that we may have to sometimes apply to our own investigative resources. What are your initial thoughts?" The Admiral rested his case.

Rupert looked at his heads of domestic and international security. For his part, the more the merrier, and if Admiral Walker vouched for the man then he was hardly likely to quibble with his judgement. "All off the record, of course?" checked the career politician.

Admiral Walker smiled; Rupert was obviously learning fast. "Naturally, Prime Minister."

The PM started collecting his papers. "Fine with me," he confirmed.

Jessica looked the Admiral square in the face. "Gordon." Both the PM and the head of MI5 were taken aback by the use of the Admiral's first name, but understood it hadn't been used lightly. "You need to make sure that you keep him on some sort of a leash. From my perspective, I am willing to take help from any quarter and I know the man and his guys are very capable, so you have my vote."

"Thank you." The Admiral turned his gaze to the head of MI5. "Charlie, what do you think?"

"Not sure I have an awful lot of choice," came the response with a half-hearted smile. "Not entirely happy, but I know he's a good guy to have on your team. So I'm OK with it too."

"Good, that's decided then. I'll call him now." The Admiral rose from his chair and made for the door. As he left, he turned to the other people in the room who were still seated. "Thank you, I believe it was the right decision."

935 Pennsylvania Avenue – Monday, Lunchtime

"Goddammit Jerry, what the fuck have your guys been up to?" Steve Brewer, Director of the FBI, was in a foul mood. He was doing his best to walk a hole into the deep carpet which bedecked his expansive place of work; the FBI's head office situated in Washington. This telephone call with the lead agent handling the bombings was turning out to be as unproductive as the rest of the calls that he had been making, and indeed taking, that morning. He needed some tangible progress as he really didn't relish another roasting at the hands of the President. The last discussion they'd had thirty minutes earlier, thanks in no small part to the paltry information that he'd been able so far to provide, had ended with the President kindly tearing him a new arsehole. He had no wish to repeat the experience.

"Steve." The two men had worked together for many years and were friends as well as work colleagues. Jerry knew his boss must have been getting a real going over for letting these two outrages happen on his watch. "As far as Boston is concerned, we've established that the plane was brought down by a shoulder-launched SAM of Japanese manufacture. Our best guess is that it was fired from a boat or dry land somewhere near the end of the runway."

"OK, so looking for a fucking vehicle is going to be like looking for the proverbial needle. What leads on the boat option?" fired back the Director.

"Nothing as yet, only good news was that there weren't many ship movements in the bay that morning so we're taking a good look at what was recorded on the harbour radar log." Jerry Black was sitting in the FBI offices in Boston; he'd been the senior 'duty officer' on call when the news of the first attack had come through. He'd flown up from Washington a couple of hours earlier, en route he had received the news about the West Coast bombing so had set up another command post there whilst in the air. The whole Boston area had been locked down and they had in similar fashion to their European counterparts put feelers out wherever possible to try to get a lead on who had shot the plane down.

Steve stopped pacing and dropped himself into the chair behind his desk. Leaning forward onto his elbows, he moved on and, addressing the speaker phone, enquired of his number two about progress on the West Coast. "So what's the latest from San Fran?" He was struggling to come to terms with a plane being shot down by SAM and then some crazy terrorist blowing up the Golden Gate Bridge. It was like something out of a Hollywood disaster movie.

Jerry could be heard to take another toke out of his cigarette. "It's a fucking mess, boss. The traffic cameras show a guy driving this huge truck up onto the bridge, parking it up, and then three or four minutes later - boom! The bridge has gone."

"Spare me the description, Jerry, it's all over the TV stations. What do we know about the truck?" The Director of the FBI had half a dozen TV screens dotted around his office, all of them either showing the plane wreckage sticking out of the bay in Boston or the space once filled by the iconic Golden Gate Bridge. The European bombings were now only making the odd brief appearance as the US audience clearly had more interest in what was happening on the domestic front rather than several thousand miles away.

"There were no plates on it as it came past the cameras and the divers haven't been able to get anything up to look at yet. Apparently the currents are ludicrously strong through that body of water. It's going to take ages before we manage to get the truck up, but we're guessing there isn't much left of it judging by the size of the charges used." Jerry wished he had more useful information to impart but acknowledged that, given the current state of confusion, he had nothing in reality but speculation to pass on.

"OK, got it. Thanks Jerry, let me know what turns up." Steve pushed the button on the speakerphone and the call was cut. He looked out through his bombproof windows onto the busy street. *Christ, what a mess*, he thought. He'd been in the service since completing a fifteen year stint in the military; at least when he'd been in the army it was much easier to know who the enemy was. Chasing terrorists was a completely different game. For all he knew the very people responsible for the bombing were, right now, down on the street outside his office.

His desk phone rang quietly.

"Yep, Darcy what is it?" snapped the Director. Whilst the general population of the USA was not likely to get to animated about terrorist events in Europe, the Director was anything but complacent about the outrages across the pond; he knew better than most that the events over the last few hours were almost certainly interconnected. Terrorism in Europe was not unheard of; the US had for the most part fortunately not experienced widespread outrages such as London had. The planes crashing into the Twin Towers had been a terrible wake up call for America; it was his job to make sure something akin to this never happened again. He had clearly failed.

One of his many personal assistants, Darcy Bailey, replied, "Director, I've got a call from an Admiral Walker in London. Says you know him and he's been holding for a while. Do you want to take the call?"

"Sure, put him though." *I wonder what the old fox wants*, he thought He had a long history with Admiral Walker. Steve held the man in high regard and valued his judgement, but also was well aware that he wasn't always as transparent as he might be. Still, that came with the territory, didn't it?

"Director, this is Gordon Walker. Thank you for taking my call, I imagine you must be extremely busy." For his part, the Admiral liked Steve Brewer and considered him a consummate professional.

"You got that right Gordon, long time no speak. What can I do for you on such a fabulous day?" He took a look out across Washington, it had started to rain.

"Director ..."

"You can drop that Director shit too, we're a bit too old for that. Come on, Gordon, what's on your mind?"

In London, the Admiral allowed himself a small smile. Typical of the Director to cut to the chase and get down to business. "Steve, we're not making much progress our end and I wanted to know if you chaps had any leads?"

"Big fat zip, Gordon. Nothing, nada, of note. President is going ape and put us on DEFCON 2 just to keep us all on our toes. It being election year and all, he's not going to miss any chance to ramp things up to show what a great leader he is in times of crisis." It was clear to the Director of the FBI that the incumbent President was not beyond making sure that he was going to score highly in the public opinion stakes. The economy was struggling, along with the rest of the developed nations, and a crisis of this nature would turn the spotlight away from what was frankly a pretty poor track record on the domestic front.

"Similar story here I'm afraid. Look. I need a favour." *Here we go*, thought the Director of the FBI, *the real reason for the call.* "We're sending over one of our guys, a man called Max Thatcher, to take a look at the Boston and San Francisco atrocities to see if he can find anything out that can shed any light on what's happened here. I'd like you to make sure he gets some help when he arrives."

The Director of the FBI was no fool; no way would the wily old fox that Admiral Walker was be calling him only for this. "And ...?" he asked.

"Max is a contractor, he has pretty unorthodox means and he's not a great believer in long drawn out legal processes, if you get my drift." Admiral Walker noted the slight pause before the response came.

"So you want me to turn a blind eye to doing things by the book and protecting civil liberties and human rights etc? That about it?" Many times in the past Steve would have liked to take a slightly less prescriptive path in terms of investigate approach.

"Yes," confirmed the Admiral

"And he'll share anything he finds?" enquired the Director innocently.

"Absolutely." The Admiral almost involuntarily crossed his fingers behind his back on that little white lie.

"I bet ... anyway we've nothing to lose. When does your man arrive?" Steve knew he would have to keep someone close to this 'contractor' if he wasn't going to be left behind on the information flow.

"He'll be in Boston later tonight." Admiral Walker was relieved with the pragmatic approach. "Thanks."

"Sure, no problem. What are friends for?" The Director of the FBI cut the call.

He dialled Jerry Black's number. "Our special friends the Brits are sending over an independent contractor to help out on the investigation. Make sure you stick someone on him and keep close to what he does."

"Why on earth would we need their help?" As far as the man in Boston was concerned he had all the resources on the ground that he needed with state-of-the-art analytical support at beck and call.

"Firstly because I said it's OK, and secondly right now we have diddly shit." The Director was in no mood for a long debate. "I'll take any help that I can get, and I know the man he's sending by reputation."

"OK, who is he?" asked Jerry

"Max Thatcher, the man who sorted the Gatekeeper business. Take care of it OK?"

"Sure thing." End of debate, the line went dead. Jerry looked over at one of the agents in the command room. "Find me a babysitter." *This could be interesting*, he thought.

Boston – Monday Night

Max hadn't taken much persuading to get involved in helping to try to find the perpetrators of the wicked crimes that had been committed during the day. He'd taken a call from Admiral Walker earlier that afternoon, and then convened a meeting with those of his team who were in the London office. As usual, once Max had laid out what information had so far come to light, it was down to Patrick to help join up the various dots and come up with a strategy.

As Max walked through the deserted airport he replayed in his mind the discussion from earlier.

~

"So what do we know so far?" Patrick posed a rhetorical question; he was standing in front of the whiteboard in the largest meeting room. Also present in addition to Max were Gregory, Pete, Fiona and Francois, who had been working on a project in London on behalf of one of Falcon Services' French clients.

"Bombing in London – military grade high explosives. Same for Paris. A rocket launcher in Boston and what would appear to be an enormous fertilizer based bomb on the West Coast. Obvious connection being the military connotations."

"Patrick, anyone with enough money could get hold of this gear," observed Gregory. The work that he and Max had so recently completed in Germany had confirmed just how easy it was to go shopping for munitions.

"True, but it's not simply getting hold of the material, mate. You need to know what to do with it; wrapping high explosive up in nails, launching SAMs and rigging four tonne fertiliser bombs is no mean feat. So I'm thinking that whoever is behind this has some military experience." From what Patrick had so far managed to piece together, the operations had been executed efficiently and the linked timings indicated a coordinated series of activities.

"OK, I'll buy that for now," stated Max, "but that doesn't narrow the field down that much. What else do you see as the connection points?"

Patrick turned his attention to the white board. "The randomness. London, Paris and Boston all resulted in significant loss of life amongst the civilian population. The Golden Gate bridge bombing killed, thankfully, only a handful of people but took out an iconic landmark which to me was more of a statement than anything."

"How do you mean?" asked Pete.

Patrick continued. "If whoever did these things wanted to have killed a lot of people in San Francisco, then why not wait a few hours until it was rush hour? No, blowing up the bridge was simply showing us what could have been done, whilst at the same time leaving us in no doubt of the capabilities of the group."

"Patrick, I don't see the 'group' angle. If there was a group behind this then why hasn't anybody claimed responsibility? It's almost as though the terrorist world are also in a state of shock themselves." Max was perplexed along with everybody else as to why no one had claimed the dubious honour of having carried out these terrible pieces of handiwork.

"I agree with Max. This doesn't have the feel of a terrorist group." Francois had been in the employ of Falcon Services for the last six years, since finishing his last tour of duty with the French Foreign Legion where he had seen firsthand the work of various terrorist groups. But nothing on this scale.

"I don't see this as the work of a closely aligned group but rather a series of groups that have been brought together to operate as one unit," explained Patrick. "There must be some central controlling element. I agree that had this all been carried out by one single group then we would by now have someone claiming it was them. The fact that we're not getting any more that the odd faction saying that the French, British and Americans are simply reaping what they've sown suggests to me at least that the 'typical' terrorist groups don't know who's behind it either.

"So if we take this thought process on a little further, we are left with the conclusion that we have witnessed has been the work of a 'virtual' terrorist organisation."

"Sorry mate, you're losing me again." Greg stated how he, along with the rest of the people in the room, was struggling to fully grasp where Patrick's train of thought was going.

"No problem, and of course I may be entirely wrong. The bombings all occurred in a comparatively short space of time; do we at least agree that these were coordinated?" asked Patrick.

Everyone in the room nodded in unison. "Go on, Patrick," encouraged Max.

The acting CEO of Falcon Services sought confirmation on his next assumption. "Do we agree that the attacks were well thought out and most likely not amateur attacks?"

Again the room was in full agreement.

"In which case, each event was handled by a 'professional' cell." There being no objections, Patrick pressed on. "So we can rule out one large organisation backing all their own cells as they would by now have bragged how clever they were. Which then leads us, or at least me, back to the conclusion that the cells were totally disconnected. They did not share a common objective but yet were all pulled together for today's fireworks by someone or a group of people with a common cause which they are yet to reveal to us all."

Max couldn't find fault with the logic. "So where do we start to find this group or individual?"

"From the information the Admiral has given us, I don't believe we're going to find much in the UK until they manage to get all the wreckage out of the river. It's going to take days to sieve through the CCTV footage. And my suspicion is they'll never be able to put the bomber back together, so I wouldn't be looking for a break in London any time soon," stated the former SBS intelligence operative.

"Where then, Patrick? We can't sit around and do nothing," said Greg.

"Please, let me finish. I understand from Gerard that in Paris they have caught a bit of a break and have got CCTV for 35-40 potential bomb carriers and they're working through these to see if that leads them somewhere. In the US the West Coast bombing is going to be hard to progress until they recover any wreckage from the bay. Frankly that could take several days, given the currents. Which leaves Boston.

"The CoastGuard have pretty good surveillance capabilities along the coast and have, according to my sources, got a couple of possible leads. Assumes of course that the rocket was launched from a boat, but that is a pretty good guess I reckon."

"So what's the suggestion, Patrick?" asked Max.

"We send Greg and Francois to Paris and you head off to Boston. I'll keep tabs on any developments here." There being no other better suggestions, the meeting was wrapped up and Max headed for the airport whilst the French away team headed for the train.

~

Max walked through the arrivals concourse at Logan Airport and made his way out towards the taxi rank.

The temperature had dropped and it was threatening to snow. Just before he was about to climb into a taxi, a stranger approached him. "Mr. Thatcher?"

"Yes, that's me." Max stopped and put his travelling bag down.

A good looking slim woman in her early forties stretched out her hand. "Gina Bourne, FBI. Steven Brewer, the Director, has asked that I help you in any way possible with your investigations." She showed him her ID badge.

Max's giant hand reached out and gently shook the proffered hand. "Please call me Max. Lovely weather."

"Please follow me, my car is just over there." She pointed in the direction of one of the No Waiting zones at a black Mercedes coupe.

Picking up his bag he followed Gina to the waiting vehicle. "Company cars are improving then," quipped Max.

"Actually it's my own. I don't get let out into the field very often and saves on the paperwork if I just claim for the mileage. Where would you like to go?" replied Gina. Max had a sinking feeling that he had been allocated a desk-based operative with minimal if any field experience, but was prepared to give her the benefit of the doubt.

They climbed in to the car; Max threw his light travelling case onto the small seats in the back. "Let's head over to the Atlantis Marina, seems a good a place as any to start."

"Sure, no problem." Gina fired up the 3.5L Mercedes and headed out of the airport onto to I90 for the short drive around the bay to the marina. The FBI agent and Max made polite small talk on the drive along the shoreline. The traffic was light and it only took them fifteen minutes to arrive at their destination.

In truth, there was not much to be seen in terms of helping solve the conundrum of who had perpetrated the attack; firstly, it was dark, and secondly, the whole area was cordoned off to prevent people coming to sight see. Not that they or any sick 'disaster tourists' were spoilt for choice in terms of seeing the consequences of the attack, as the whole bay was lit up by spotlights covering the water where the jet had crashed. There were naval ships covering almost every inch of water, interspersed with heavy lifting gear perched on barges brought in to lift the remnants of the Delta commuter jet.

Parking the car on the edge of the closed off zone around the Marina, they made their way down to the water's edge to get a better perspective on how the airliner might have been brought down. All too easy was Max's immediate impression.

"What sort of security is there around here normally?" he asked his guide.

"Frankly not a lot, Max. After the Twin Towers we stepped up security all over the place, but I guess over time we've become a bit more complacent."

He scanned the area. "There are so many possible places to launch from around here that if someone were determined to let loose with a shoulder-launched device, you'd never stop them in my opinion. Frankly I'm surprised it hasn't been done before." He bent down under the police's No Entry tape and walked along the pontoon where half a dozen small boats were moored up.

"Hey mister, you can't go in there!" shouted one of the policeman milling around the area.

"It's OK, he's with me." Gina flashed her FBI badge at the cop making his way over to confront Max. "What do you think, Max?"

"I'm not sure we're going to be able to make much headway here. I imagine your guys have had a good look, have they found anything?" Max turned around and studied the buildings around the marina itself. Any of them, he considered, would make a decent place to use as a firing point. Intuitively he preferred the theory that the attack had taken place from the water, to his mind there was even less chance of being spotted and then it was an easy matter of disappearing off into the poorly lit waters of the bay.

"I'm afraid not. No trace of anything untoward. From what we can tell, the perp could have launched from anywhere in a quarter mile radius of this point." Gina was frustrated with the lack of progress all round; a common complaint shared by the many hundreds of men and women now working around the world to try and find the people behind the atrocities. She had initially been delighted to have been selected for some field work but was coming rapidly to the conclusion that she was simply there to take notes.

They had had a brief conversation with one of the many FBI agents working on the ground, but that had provided little additional information. Max was coming to the conclusion there wasn't much to be learned at the scene itself.

Max pulled his jacket a little tighter around his shoulders and headed back the way they had come towards Gina's parked car. "Shall we head back to the hotel?"

The FBI agent hadn't known what to expect from Max. She had read a file on him that described some of his work in the Special Forces and how he had set up his own security business. There was some reference to the Gatekeeper incident but the notes only referred to another file for which she didn't have the requisite security clearance. The man was polite to a fault, but so far had not given much up in terms of information or explained where his thought processes were taking his thinking. She was, frankly, disappointed, and wanted more. "How about a quick beer on the way back?" she asked, regretting instantly how the question came out. It almost sounded as she wanted to flirt with him.

"Sure, why not?" Max said with an easy smile.

They drove for about twenty minutes back into the centre of Boston and found an Irish pub just off State Street.

"What'll it be?" asked the bartender. It was fairly late and there were only a few hardened drinkers left in the bar enjoying Jimi Hendrix's version of 'All Along The Watchtower'; one of Max's favourite tunes, as it happened.

"Beer and a shot of bourbon," replied Gina, Max sat himself beside her at the bar and nodded to the barman. "Same, please."

The drinks arrived. "Cheers," said Max, raising his frosted beer glass and clinked it against Gina's before taking a decent gulp.

Using the back of her had to wipe her mouth in a less than ladylike manner, Gina asked, "So Max how did you end up working for the British Government on this particular project?"

Max noted that subtlety probably was not that high up on Gina's skills-to-be-learnt agenda. "Not a lot to tell in truth Gina, my work brings me into contact a lot with various government agencies including your own. No one is making much progress on the bombings and the guys in London thought I may be able to help." He took a nip from the whisky shot in front of him and followed it up with another drink from the beer glass.

Gina followed suit on the drinking front; the whisky burned her throat on the way down but left a lovely warm sensation in her stomach.

"Same again?" The highly attendant barman was back.

"Sure," replied the FBI agent. Max was obviously happy not to force the conversation, so Gina decided on seeing if he would open up another front.

"So Max, perhaps you could give me a bit of insight into what ..." the rest of her sentence was cut short as three heavyset men came crashing in through the bar's front door. The leader of the drunken party rolled up to the bar and instructed the barman, in badly slurred words, to pour three beers.

"Guys, I think you've probably had enough," probably wasn't the most engaging line that the man behind the bar could have come up with.

"Shut it, man, and pour the fucking beer!" His two colleagues stood alongside their main man and indicated that they weren't planning on leaving any time soon. With a resigned shrug of the shoulders the bartender went off to pour the beer; he wasn't going to argue with three of them.

Turning his attention to Gina, the leader of the pack breathed alcoholic fumes over the FBI agent. "And what's your name missy? My name is Paul and these are my good buddies Chuck and Davy."

Gina smiled sweetly. "Really, how nice." She turned her back, indicating that the short conversation was at an end.

"Looks like you crashed and burned there, Paul," said one of his drinking partners.

"Go fuck yourself, Chuck." Paul moved around so that he stood between Max and Gina. "Now that's not very nice, young lady. How about you tell me your name and we start again?"

Max turned from his sitting position and looked at the unwelcome guest. "Paul - it is Paul, right?"

"Yeah, so what of it?" said the man, now squaring up to Max.

"I think it would be a good idea if you and your mates left the nice lady alone, took your beers over into the corner, drank them quickly and left."

"Why don't you go fuck yourself, you limey prick." Paul had spotted Max's accent and was entirely confident in being able to take care of the lady's 'date', especially as he would be backed up by his other pals.

Paul's two friends came across and stood behind where Max was sitting. The former Special Forces operative stood up; if things were going to turn rough, he didn't want to be sitting down.

"Max, leave it." Gina reached inside her bag and was about to flash her FBI badge when Paul decided that he was going to teach the Brit a lesson. He swung his beer glass towards Max's face.

"Get him, guys." His two friends went to grab Max around the shoulders. They were far too slow.

Max easily dodged the incoming glass and, catching Paul's forearm and upper arm on the way through, used the assailant's momentum to push him in to the surprised Chuck and Davy. The three of them crashed in unison across a couple of the unoccupied bar stools next to where Max had been sitting. Chuck picked himself up and went for Max; he was stopped dead his tracks by a hard right elbow to the side of the head. Paul and Davy threw themselves against Max's hard torso; the group fell back on to the floor. Max quickly broke free and was up on his feet facing the two other men, who had got up somewhat more slowly.

"Last chance, boys," said Max.

Gina had her badge out and was screaming, "FBI," at the top of her voice but no one seemed to want to hear her. Paul lunged towards Max, but before he had covered half the distance between them Max had delivered a hard and well-placed kick to the man's testicles. As Paul doubled up in agony clutching his lower region, Max smashed the man's face with his right knee. He fell to the floor with blood pouring from his face.

"Behind you, Max!" Gina called out as Chuck picked up one of the bar room stools. Max spun round and drove his shoulder into the oncoming attacker, knocking him back towards the bar. The stool was dropped behind the bar as Max knocked the wind out of Chuck; grabbing him by the collar, he ended Chuck's evening with a 'Glaswegian kiss' timed to perfection and placed neatly across the bridge of the man's nose.

Davy jumped on Max's back only to be met with a vicious elbow into his rib cage. The pain from the force of the impact was excruciating and he let go of his grip and collapsed on the floor gasping for air. Max was about to smash a foot into the man's face, but Gina's voice cut through his consciousness. "Stop, Max, for Christ's sake you're going to kill them."

Gina looked at Max; he had hardly broken sweat and looked like nothing had happened. The three men on the floor told a different story.

Max smiled at Gina. "Well I don't know about you, but I think I've had enough excitement for the evening, shall we go to the hotel now?"

They drove back to the hotel in silence. Gina would never forget the look of pure malice in Max's eyes just before she managed to prevent him from landing the final blow on Davy. This guy was a very dangerous animal.

News 24 Studios, London South Bank – Tuesday, 06.59

The studio manager silently counted down the lead presenter and the number two as the opening credits announcing the seven o'clock news played out on screens around the world. He signalled three, two, one and pointed at the anchorman.

"Good Morning, this is Darren Porter." The camera cut across to the woman sitting on his right.

"And Maggie Black," contributed the co-anchor. Darren and Maggie had been hosting the breakfast news section for the past eighteen months. In their time in the roles they thought they had seen everything, but the news over the past twenty four hours had been nothing like they had ever experienced. The ratings for their slots had shot up as people around the globe had tuned in to get the latest information.

"The headlines for this Tuesday morning at seven am." Darren's head and shoulders were replaced by images of train carriages still lying floodlit in the river Thames, followed in turn by imagery from San Francisco, Boston and finally Paris. He had continued reading from his teleprompter. "Around the world there has been outcry and outrage expressed for the cowardice of the attacks, and there has been a coordinated crack down on known terrorist cells." The videotape showed huge piles of flowers outside Victoria station the Metro station and outside of Logan Airport. "We are expecting some more formal communiqués later today, and we'll be taking you to all the bomb sites for the latest news, but first to our lead terrorist analyst who is by the Thames just outside of Victoria Station. Jo, what have you got for us?"

Jo Lockton, her first name, shortened from Josephine much to the annoyance of her parents, was standing on Grosvenor Road on the westerly side of the railway bridge - officially named Grosvenor Bridge, but more often known as Victoria Railway Bridge. She was wrapped in a heavy coat and standing with her back to the river so that her audience could look past her and see the ongoing recovery work.

"Good morning, Darren. There is still no official word from the Government about who is responsible for these atrocities. The current death toll in London stands at over four hundred with another ninety people still in hospital, many with serious life threatening injuries. As you can see," she indicated behind her, "the recovery work is still underway, and best estimates are that it will take a further two days before they are able to recover all the carriages."

In the background the avid viewers could see the macabre scene lit up by the high intensity lights that had been brought in to turn night into day. There were a couple of heavy duty lifting cranes on the bridge itself; in addition there was a smaller support unit on a barge to assist those working in the river. The multitude of people moving around the area of the outrage provided testimony, if any were needed, to the amount of work being undertaken.

Jo continued with her narrative. "As you'll know, the Thames is still tidal at this point and this, combined with the increased water flows caused by the rain we've been having, is hampering efforts."

"Jo," it was Maggie's turn to get in on the show, "can you perhaps give us some insight to how London commuters are coping and coming to terms with yesterday's dreadful events?" Maggie Black was a very attractive looking woman; in her late thirties she had worked hard to get to her position as co-anchor for News 24. She desperately wanted to be the main lead but Darren, at least for now, appeared to have no intention of moving on. Maggie begrudgingly accepted that he had a certain gravitas that the additional ten years of experience in the limelight had taught him to use very well in these types of world events. Still, the recently increased show ratings were propelling her image more into the public gaze, and her agent had assured her that he would capitalise on the opportunities to appear on various 'this' or 'that' celebrity shows. There was money to be made, and she recognised that her good looks would, in time, fade, so she had to make the most of her chance in the spotlight.

"As you can imagine, Maggie, Victoria Station has been closed which has caused major chaos for those still willing to make the trip in. There's no news on when it will be re-opened, so in the interim commuters are being asked to come in via the other major stations on the south side of London."

"Are people returning to work?" asked Darren. From what he'd seen, most of town was pretty quiet.

"Darren, it's still fairly early to tell, but early indications are that a lot of people have decided not to run the potential gauntlet of taking a train, and stayed at home. Security has been stepped up and there are now police officers travelling on almost all commuter trains." Jo and the other news reporters had been asked by the Government to try to keep upbeat. It was important to keep the City working.

"Given your experience in this field, do you have an opinion on which organisation is responsible for these terrible events?" Darren knew of Jo's long-term fascination with terrorism, and she was recognised both nationally and internationally as something of an expert in the field.

"It's all pure speculation at this moment Darren, there's not been much forthcoming from the various Governments. As I mentioned at the top of the report, we're expecting more today but my sources have indicated that they really have little idea who the perpetrators are and what they hoped to achieve by attacking such soft targets. It's still very unclear as to whether the events have been coordinated or are the work of a single terrorist group."

"OK, thanks Jo." Maggie was now back on screen. "We'll now take you over to Sean Green in Boston for an update from there; Sean ..."

The portable high intensity spotlights that had been illuminating Jo in the gloomy morning drizzle were switched off. As was her style, she made a point of thanking her team for their professional piece of work. She checked her Cartier, a thirtieth birthday present from her parents – it wasn't her favourite, but looked good on camera. Her next report was due at nine o'clockso she had some time to kill and decided to make her way into the West End before reporting to the TV studios on the South Bank.

Traffic was light and she had to walk for about a quarter of mile towards Vauxhall Bridge before she managed to hail a taxi. "Where to, luv?" asked the driver. The cabbie had decided to make the trip in to central London despite the expectation that there would be far fewer prospective customers around than normal. He was saving to take his family away to Disneylandin the summer holidays and couldn't afford to lose a day's takings. Jo was his first fare of the morning.

"Hay's Mews, number twelve please." She settled herself in the back of the taxi and pushed the button on the side panel to get a bit of warmth in the cab. She would have liked to work through, in her mind, the events of the past twenty four hours and figure out what the authorities might be doing to pull together the full picture. She had contacts all over the place but so far they had not come up with much insightful material; it looked a really tricky problem to solve.

Unfortunately her face was well known from the TV, and it didn't take long for her driver to buck up enough courage to try and engage her in conversation. "Sorry to be impolite, miss, but aren't you the reporter from the news channel?" She could have cut him off but thought better of it; she liked an audience and got a kick out of being something of a recognised, albeit 'B' class, celebrity.

"Yes, I am. How's your day going?" That was enough of a conversation starter and the cabbie chatted away with her amicably for the fifteen minutes that it took them to cross town. It would be the highlight of his day, if not the week. It would be something noteworthy enough, certainly from his perspective, to share with his mates at the golf club on the coming weekend. He started working out in his mind how he would describe how he had been chatting with and driving the sexy Jo Lockton around for the morning.

The trip up from the river and towards the West End was made through almost deserted streets; there were hardly any traffic jams as would normally, even at that time of the morning, have been the case.

They pulled up outside the expensive mews town house. Jo reached in her purse and gave the cabbie £15 for the £10 fare. The driver was suitably delighted; *nice way to start the day*, he thought, as he pulled away from the kerb and went in search of his next fare. The cabbie reckoned he'd practise his story about driving Jo on his next fare.

Money really was of no consequence to Jo; she had plenty, and when Daddy died she'd have a load more. Other than buying clothes and other more basic commodities she had few, if any, bills to worry about. Her properties were paid for and she had a steady string of suitors all willing to foot any bills for a good night out on the town. She enjoyed the finer things in life, but wanted to find a balance and perspective with how the rest of the world lived. It was one of the reasons that she had focused on terrorism as a media journalist. Many of her assignments, along with the obvious adrenalin rush provided by the inherent danger, took her to parts of the globe where money only had superficial value. Living rough in the training camps of Africa, Arabia or in the mountains of Pakistan she had learnt quickly that who had how much money was of little consequence. People she had met there trained to fulfil far bigger objectives than just trying to get to the top of some giant money tree; their goals were typically not measured in materialistic terms.

She climbed a couple of steps up to the impressive town house entrance portal and pushed the doorbell whilst at the same time opening the door with her own key. She didn't particularly like her parents' pied-à-terre, liked even less the grandiose mansion set in the Cotswolds, and always felt a bit awkward coming to visit. She felt happiest in her open plan apartments with only very minimalist furniture for company.

Making her way across the marble floored hall, she walked into one of the mews house's front rooms which overlooked the quiet street. She hadn't expected to find anyone other than staff in occupancy; apparently this morning there were none to be seen. Her mother rarely made the trip down to London these days whilst her father busied himself in the House of Lords or with a new bit of skirt. She was quite sure that her mother knew about the various and not infrequent dalliances, but for the sake of the family name Mrs. Lockton was prepared to say and do nothing. If it had been down to the daughter, Mr. Lockton would be a gelding by now.

Josephine Caroline Lockton sat herself behind the beautifully crafted partners desk and started looking for the document that she had come across town to find. Godfrey Lockton, her father, was a professional do-nothing sort of a person. He wasn't idle as such, but he was one of those people who was very happy to leave the status quo. The property business had been kind to the family over the years, and the family fortune could probably be measured in the tens of millions of pounds. Jo had worked out privately a conservative figure might be approaching £60m.

The head of the family was a sometime Ambassador, employed when the Government couldn't find someone else to send to a career dead-end of a post. The thrusting types wanted to be in the limelight and take the large and important posts around the world. The less attractive postings were mainly window dressings and ceremonial in nature which, of course, suited Godfrey immensely. He would go and look after the locals in some far flung Caribbean island or somewhere in the Indian Ocean that no one had ever heard of or frankly could care less for.

He liked all the pomp and circumstance that came along with the postings. The total lack of having to make any meaningful decisions was a happy balance of being in the limelight, albeit on small stages, and not actually having any material responsibility to keep one awake at night. The added bonus, of course, was the occasional royal visit to far flung parts of the Commonwealth which were very jolly affairs, as the various photographs dotted around his private office could attest to.

Satisfied that neither her father nor any staff were currently in residence, Jo leant back in her father's handmade chair and, crossing her legs, placed her knee length leather boots unceremoniously on top of the highly polished wooden desk with its leather inset. She began to study the report that Godfrey had left in his unlocked drawer. Marked Top Secret, it was a detailed breakdown of the last series of COBRA meetings. Daddy's latest stint in central government was as an advisor to the Cabinet on how events, such as had recently unfolded, would impact on the far flung reaches of the once great empire. Jo frankly doubted that anyone paid him much attention, but it suited her purposes that he was copied on minutes from all the key meetings that were taking place around the Palace of Westminster.

Her father's contacts had proved invaluable over the years. Had certainly helped get her into Oxford, where she was a top class student and where she had passed her history degree with honours. His address book had got her a break into the media and then opened doors to the movers and shakers in all the most unpleasant places in the world that her father so obviously shunned.

The relationship between them had never been good and indeed had been soured from the moment of her birth when the midwife had told the expectant father that he was the proud dad of a daughter. Apparently, rather than going in to congratulate his wife and welcome the new arrival personally, Lord Lockton had turned on his heel in the waiting area outside the private room and gone off to play bridge with some of his cronies.

He had spent no time with her as a child, little more when she became able to hold a sensible conversation, and since she had decided to spend her time in the dreaded left wing media he was at best polite towards her. No, they had nothing in common. They rarely met and neither regretted this state of affairs one iota. Lord Lockton was bitterly disappointed that his wife had been unable to carry another pregnancy through to a successful conclusion and was, at least in his mind, stuck with a daughter that he didn't care much for in an industry he loathed. He had made no secret to Jo that he was greatly saddened that there was no son and heir to carry on the family name of Lockton.

Satisfied that no one in government had a clue who was behind the spate of seemingly disconnected terrorist events and that she wasn't missing out on anything, she replaced the folder and let herself out of the house. Being able to find out the inside track though her father's somewhat lax security measures had resulted in Jo being able, over the years, to break big stories ahead of the rest of the media pack.

She took a left turn out of the front door and hailed a black taxi by Berkeley Square. "South Bank Studios, please."

"Sure thing miss, hey, aren't you the lady from the news or something ...?"

Jo knew that there were going to be a lot of surprised people when all that had transpired became public; on this occasion, she decided to let the taxi driver's question stand and pretended not to have heard.

Gare du Nord, Paris – Tuesday, Mid-Morning

Greg and Francois had taken the Eurostar from St Pancras that morning, leaving Patrick and the rest of the team working on the project to collate information from the two remote teams and combine it with what sketchy information was coming out of London.

"Where to?" asked Greg.

"We'll take a taxi over to the first arrondissement and take a look around," replied Francois. "We've got a meeting early this afternoon with Gerard."

The weather was being kind that morning and had the reason for their trip not been so dire, the pair would have enjoyed finding a street cafe and sitting outside in the watery sunshine shooting the breeze and reminiscing over old times.

Francois walked purposefully out of the station and crossed over to the waiting taxi rank. "C'mon Greg, vite."

Greg jogged along behind his old friend and got in the other side of the taxi. "Bonjour, Pont Neuf, s'il vous plaît," instructed Francois.

"Bien sur."

Francois chatted away with the driver on the fifteen-minute drive through the half empty streets of Paris which, on this sombre day, was anything but gay. Greg was no linguist and he had forgotten almost all his school French, so contented himself with looking out of his window and taking in the sights of the French capital.

It was pretty clear to Greg that many of the tourists that one would normally have expected to have seen wandering around had thought better of it. They were either staying in their hotel rooms or cutting their trips short. This, combined with a marked low turnout of the normal commuter traffic, created an almost surreal effect across the normally vibrant city. Apart from the temperature, one could easily believe that one were driving through the Parisian streets at five am on a beautiful summer's morning, not approaching midday on a normal working day in the middle of January.

The taxi pulled over about a hundred yards from a taped off area surrounded by Gendarmes. Francois paid the driver and the two operatives climbed out of the vehicle and made their way over to the cordoned off area.

"What did the taxi driver have to say?" enquired Greg. Whilst he had no idea of the precise content of the discussion between the two native French speakers, he was pretty sure that Francois had not been exchanging football stories.

"Unsurprisingly he didn't have a lot to add to what we already know," said Francois.

Greg nodded; no surprise there. "Go on," he encouraged.

"I asked him what the word on the street was about who might be responsible. The favourite option appears to be the North Africans; you remember all the stuff going off in Marseille and around Toulon?"

"Vaguely," responded Greg.

Francois filled in some of the details. "There have been a lot of problems during recent times with illegal immigrants and drug smuggling down on the coast. Some of the stuff has got quite nasty; the Parisians believe this bombing to be the work of one of the drug cartels making a point to the government."

"What do you think?" Greg enquired.

"It's certainly possible, and as you saw on the drive over, it's certainly had an effect." Francois had been taken aback like Greg. His beloved Paris was a ghost town.

Greg sensed there was more. "But ...?"

"If it were the drug lords or immigration related, why no claim for having done this terrible thing?" It was more of a rhetorical question, and as Greg didn't have a sensible answer to the question posed, he kept his thoughts to himself.

"Let's ask around and see if we can find any more out before we meet up with Gerard," suggested Francois.

"Guess you'll be asking most of the questions then!" Greg replied with a smile.

Boston – Tuesday, 07.10

Max finished showering; in his reflection in the full length mirror he could see that he had picked up a couple of bruises from last night's festivities. Walking out of the bathroom, he looked out of his functional if not luxurious room at Seaport Boston Hotel. The view even in the half-light was pretty special. The hotel was located right on the waterfront with an uninterrupted view out over the bay to Logan Airport. The authorities had wanted to ensure that normality returned as quickly as possible and, with no damage to the airport's infrastructure itself, had insisted that it reopen. As he completed getting dressed, Max could see planes landing and taking off in the distance. Heaven knows whether the flights carried any passengers; he doubted that they were in any event overly busy. The view out of the small aeroplane windows as they passed over where the recovery operation was still in full flow would not have instilled much confidence.

He took a quick look at his iPhone to see whether any new news had been forthcoming whilst he had slept: nothing. Checking his watch, he noted that he had ten minutes to get downstairs and meet his 'host', Gina, for breakfast. He was under no illusions that Gina's primary role was to babysit him and make sure that anything he found out was passed on immediately, if not sooner, to the Director of the FBI. No problem, he thought, as long as she didn't hold him back too much.

Max crossed the lobby and found Gina waiting in the self-service restaurant. "Morning Max did you sleep well?" She looked good, dressed in a smart grey trouser suit. Max still took pleasure out of looking at women but had not, at this juncture, had the heart to want to get involved with another partner. It was too soon and his emotions still too raw; he had decided that would give himself a little time to complete the healing process.

"Very well, thank you Gina. How about you?" Max sat himself opposite the FBI agent. The room was only half full and Max would have bet that the majority were from the various press corps that had descended on the city in the wake of the bombing.

"Yes fine too, thanks." Gina had had a good opportunity to study Max as he had walked across the hotel lobby. She thought better of bringing up last night's fight in the bar; it hadn't appeared to phase Max at all, and seemed a closed matter as far as he was concerned. *A very good looking guy*, she thought, and from the brief exchanges before the melee last night he seemed a nice guy. He moved with natural easy athleticism and was clearly very capable of looking after himself. Max would be a good catch, she reckoned, but there was something in his eyes. She had seen it all too clearly the night before, which made her recognise that he was a lethal machine ready to go into action without great provocation. He was friendly enough but he was somehow remote and cold. His eyes, if indeed they were windows into his soul, were dark pools of malice most of the time with only the odd flash of warmth.

Pleasantries exchanged, Max made his way over to the self-service buffet bar and helped himself to a less than healthy breakfast of hash browns, Canadian bacon, small beef sausages and beans. He skipped the grits, never having quite got the taste of them. Returning to the table, he noted that Gina had satisfied herself with some yoghurt and fruit.

"What's the plan for the day, Max?" asked Gina.

"I rather thought this was your back yard and you might help me get started," replied Max easily.

"Look, Max, I'm not sure why your guys thought sending you over here is such a good idea. We've got everything under control. So I'll take to anywhere you want to go, but I'm expecting you to lead and I'll happily follow and facilitate." Obviously she wasn't planning on giving too much away, and was looking for Max to let on what he did and didn't know. She had hoped to open him up a little last night but the run in with Paul and his pals had scuppered that plan.

"Gina, please can we cut to the chase and get some ground rules agreed." He was in no mood to mess around with the politics between the UK and USA. "I'm here to do a job. It's a job I'm pretty good at. I have no interest in whose jurisdiction we're in. To me the ONLY thing that matters is finding the bastards who have done this." He paused for effect and to make sure that Gina was getting the message.

Happy that she was at least paying attention, he carried on. "I need to you to tell me everything you know, I will happily reveal all that I know. Once we've done that, we'll make a plan of action, OK?"

"Sounds reasonable" agreed Gina. She liked his direct style; he may be cold but she knew intuitively that she could trust the man sitting opposite her implicitly. Max had that effect on people.

He gave her a big smile. "Good, now perhaps whilst I work my way through this heart-stopping breakfast you could fill me in on what you know?"

Gina pulled out eight thin manila folders from her bag under the table. "These are the short list of names that we came up with from the Coast Guard, they represent all the boats that were moving in the harbour at that time of day. We've interviewed them all and drawn a blank."

Max looked up from his breakfast and finished the mouthful he had been working on. "OK, let's go through them again if you wouldn't mind."

London – Tuesday, Lunchtime

"Patrick, this is Admiral Walker." He was sitting in his office in the Admiralty buildings sited along the Mall in the centre of London a stone's throw from Trafalgar Square. He was tired and in need of some good news. Just over twenty four hours after the Victoria bombing and so far there were no leads.

Patrick was pacing around the top floor of the Falcon Services building in Chiswick, West London. The former intelligence officer had converted the main meeting room into a large operations centre. There were flip chart sheets pinned all over the walls with photos attached and centre stage, on the main whiteboard, there was a huge diagram with as yet few connecting lines.

"Good morning, Admiral." He took a quick look at his watch. "Oops, lunchtime already. Where does the time go?" Patrick was tired; he had had only a couple of hours' sleep since Max had received the Admiral's call yesterday asking for their help. With no family commitments and only a string of occasional female friends-with-benefits to distract him, he was a workaholic.

"How are you guys getting on?" enquired the Admiral.

"Nothing material to report yet, sir. We've sent a team to Paris and I'm waiting for an update. Max is in Boston, early morning there. From the email he sent last night I understand he's been to the crash site but that didn't help our investigation much."

"OK, appreciate it's early days but we need to make some progress on this pronto." The Admiral was conscious that the length of rope which had been extended him to bring in Max could just as easily be withdrawn if nothing was forthcoming.

"Understood sir," Patrick confirmed. "Do you have anything for us, sir?"

"Not a great deal I'm afraid, forensics believe that the explosives came from a batch that ought to be in Afghanistan and not being used to blow up a commuter train in Central London. Our guys in MI5 concur with your view that the bomb was detonated remotely, so we're checking the CCTV from the traffic cameras in the area." It never ceased to amaze him how such dangerous materials could suddenly 'disappear' when they were supposed to be under lock and key.

"That's interesting; I wouldn't be surprised if the French bomb material was from the same source." Patrick was well aware of how pieces of kit were supposedly lost or ordnance not correctly accounted for. "Has that information been shared with the French?"

"I believe so. Presumably that helps us a bit?" Admiral Walker was frankly desperate for a break in the case.

"It all helps fill in the puzzle. If we can narrow down the likely source that might help lead us to whomever was ultimately supplied to. The problem, as you well know Admiral, is there is a huge market in this type of material and given there are 'live' conflicts all over the place, it's comparatively easy for people to get hold of the material. Anyway thanks for the update, I'll let you know when Max drops us an update from the US," confirmed Patrick.

"Thanks." Admiral Walker pressed the button his speakerphone to end the call.

Patrick had chosen not to say anything on the call, but the Admiral's comment about a consignment of high explosives going missing in Afghanistan rang a bell with him. He left the meeting room come operations centre and went back to his office. He wasn't sure, but he had a feeling that he had recently read in a file about Semtex and a distribution business in Western Europe. He sat down and pulled up the central company database as he thought. Max's latest mission in Hamburg. There could be a connection.

"Helga, wie geht's?" Patrick had called the head of the BvF in Hamburg. Helga Evers had worked for the BvF her entire career; in her late forties, she was a professional spinster. Her heavyset features didn't enamour her easily to any potential suitors and this, combined with her famously very direct approach to life, ensured her marital status was unlikely to change any time soon.

"Sehr gut, Patrick, und dir?" She was sitting in her office overlooking the Binnenalster.

"Yes, very well thanks. Look I need some information about Herr Blick and some of his recent transactions."

"No problem, I'll help if I can." She was very grateful that Max had brought her team in very early on the work that Falcon Services had been contracted for.

"You'll obviously know about the bombings in London, Paris and the two in America?"

"Ja, terrible business," confirmed the head of the BvF.

"We need to try and find out whether young Herr Blick had a hand in supplying the bomb material, and I seemed to remember that on one of the bill of lading reports there was reference to Semtex. Could you take a quick look for me?" requested Patrick.

"Sure, hang on a minute please." Helga opened up a new window on her desktop computer and clicked on the central document repository. Entering her password, she started studying the documents which had been scanned onto the system.

She picked out a couple of data fields. "Patrick there's a reference to a contact called Blake, certainly looks like it could be Semtex involved. The notes suggest this was stolen military munitions. Is that helpful?"

"A little, what information is there about this 'Blake'?" Patrick waited whilst he could hear Helga tapping away on her keyboard.

"We have no more on Blake. Just a name on a file, sorry." She was disappointed not to have been able to help more.

"OK, thanks. Look, if you find any more on the customer it could be very helpful."

"Sure, no problem. Tschuss."

Patrick sat back in his chair. *Ummm,* he thought, *a name but no more.*

Boston – Tuesday, Morning

The pair had spent an hour and a half going through the eight detailed reports that had been compiled by the FBI, and Max had cut the potential list of suspects to only a couple that he believed had any mileage. He didn't doubt that the FBI and local police had been thorough, but was keen to go and ask the two men on the list a few questions of his own.

Max sat in the passenger seat of Gina's smart convertible Mercedes as they made their way south down I93 towards Weymouth. From the update Gina had given him over breakfast, the local police and FBI were concentrating their efforts around the Marina itself. The consensus was now that the rocket had in fact been launched from dry land and not a boat. The Coast Guard had checked out the various boat movements in the bay; none, as they had discussed over breakfast, had turned up any hot leads, so the focus had returned to checking on CCTV traffic camera footage and the Marina's own security systems.

"So Gina, how did you end up working for the FBI?" Max had been idly playing with the radio and had settled on a local light rock station.

"Nothing terribly exciting, I'm afraid. I graduated from business school down in Columbia, South Carolina, and was looking for a career in investment banking. I had done a lot of work in analytics and mathematics is something of a strength of mine." Max looked across at Gina. At five foot ten, a brunette with olive eyes and a well-trained body, she was certainly very attractive. He wasn't surprised that she was highly intelligent; she had a quiet confidence and the FBI were pretty picky about who they recruited.

"So how did the secret service lure you away from a lucrative career in banking?" enquired Max.

Gina turned her attention briefly away from the road and looked across at Max. "Off the record?"

This could be interesting, Max thought. "Sure, my lips are sealed."

"I had been working for one of the big investment banks for a couple of years, you may have heard of them, Boulder Corp?" Max nodded confirming that he had; he remembered something in the news a few years back.

"I was working in the overseas settlements area on some pretty convoluted treasury bill based derivatives and I found some irregularities," explained Gina.

From memory Max was beginning to put the rest of the story together. "Were you involved in that business with the Russians and the Cayman Islands scam?"

"Yes, I discovered how they were laundering billions of dollars through offshore trusts and how certain members of the bank had been complicit in the transactions."

Max took an appreciative look across at the woman driving the car. *Gutsy lady,* he mused. "Can't imagine that made you the most popular person around the trading desks."

Gina smiled. "No, that would be something of an understatement. I took what I had found out to my boss and he did nothing. As it turned out, he was a small cog in the whole machine, but he obviously got word to some of the bigger fish who made it very clear that unless I forgot what I had seen, I might not get to enjoy a full and happy life."

Max nodded. "That must have been scary." He was well aware of the types of people that were involved in this scale of financial skulduggery. Not nice people, and perfectly willing to kill to keep these types multi-billion dollar businesses going. "How did you fix the problem?"

"I went and talked to my father about the problem. He was an ex-marine and was all for finding the people who were threatening me and shooting them on the spot. Good old dad!" Gina allowed herself a rueful smile. "Anyway when we had agreed that route one might not be the best alternative, he looked up some of his old colleagues from the army. Eventually he found one that was working for the FBI."

From the description, Max liked her father immediately. "Go on, what happened when the FBI got involved?"

"They set me up with a wiretap, this allowed us to get a couple of the junior players on tape threatening me and then we tried to put together a trap to ensnare the big fish." Max seemed to recall there were few arrests. "Anyway, the second half of the plan didn't quite work out. We stopped the transactions, but the people behind the scam must have heard us coming as they evaporated into thin air."

"I'm guessing that after this had all gone through it would have been hard for you to go back to work for the bank?"

"You got it. I was a heroine for a little while but that turned rapidly into being labelled as a whistleblower and a potential 'spy in the camp'." Gina paused for a moment to collect her thoughts. "I couldn't stay with the bank and frankly I was unemployable anywhere else. Luckily for me the FBI kindly then offered me a role as an analyst and that's how I end up being where I am today."

Max could sense her righteous disappointment for how the bank would have treated her back then. Even though what she did was very courageous he could imagine that her erstwhile employers would have preferred for the whole matter to stay out of the public domain. "I'm very impressed," he said with due sincerity.

Gina was keen to return the discussions to the subject in hand. "Max, I don't want to appear to be negative but why are we heading off to Weymouth when everyone else is hunting for the suspects back in Boston?" She turned off I93 onto Hancock Street to make the seven or eight mile run down along the coast to Hingham Shipyard, which doubled as a popular place to spend the weekend as well as a small fishing harbour.

"Precisely because everyone is looking somewhere else," Max answered somewhat cryptically. "You've got top flight guys on the ground, Gina, but I believe they are looking, in their mind, for a known organisation. From what we've put together in London, we believe that the various bombings are not the work of a single group."

"How so?" Gina's FBI pass clearly gave her carte blanche regarding the local speed limits, and she accelerated hard past a group of slow moving traffic.

"A single group would have claimed responsibility, most likely could not have kept the planning secret and by now one of the secret service entities would have got a sniff of who was behind it." Max took a look out of the window at the scenery flashing by. "Nice part of the world. Never had much cause to visit, so only know downtown."

"Yeah, it's nice but very pricey." Gina had little interest in playing the tour guide and returned to her theme of what on earth they were doing away from where all the action was taking place. "So what's the interest with the guy in Hingham and the other in Weymouth? They both checked out. And why them and not the other half a dozen people we've interviewed?"

"Gina, I can't be sure until we meet the men whether there is anything untoward, but from the reports we went through both look a little too pat," explained Max.

"Pat?" Not a term she was familiar with.

"It means all a little too innocent and well-explained. Verging on contrived would be my opinion. Anyway, we'll find out soon enough."

Gina stopped at a major intersection, waited for the lights to allow her to pull across the main road and drove down the aptly named - judging by the businesses that they passed - Shipyard Drive. They stopped by the waterfront at the front of a fairly modern building whose facade told them in bold letters that they were in the right place for Stern and Sons Boat Builders.

Max climbed out of the car and just before they made it across the parking lot turned to face the FBI agent. He gently reached out for her arm. "Gina, I would appreciate it if you let handle the interview ... OK?"

"Sure thing, Max." Gina remained convinced that they were in the wrong place and were wasting her time. It was fine with her if Max wanted to kick tyres, but she felt that she was being left behind from the main investigative work. She had spent literally no time in the field and when the offer of helping a British secret agent had been put to her, she couldn't help believe that this was going to be a bit more exciting than her daily desk-bound analysis work.

Even in the short time that she had spent in his company, she had come to like Max as an individual and, despite herself, couldn't help but be physically attracted to him. This morning's decision to go south and away from the crime scene appeared to confirm her fears that, frankly, it now looked like she was doing purely a babysitting job, and that didn't sit all that well with her.

They walked into the building, the front half of which was a veritable emporium of boating and fishing equipment. Max casually looked around the various goodies on show; his background in the Navy and love of the sea meant that he was well aware of all the uses of the items on display. *Nice gear*, he mused, *all top quality and priced accordingly.*

Max strode purposefully up to the main counter and asked the young female checkout assistant whether the owner's son was around.

"He's out back mister, can I help with you anything?" She flashed him a big smile.

"My name is Max Thatcher and this is my colleague FBI Agent Bourne, he's expecting us." He returned the warm smile.

Suitably impressed and intrigued in equal measure, she happily replied, "Oh sure, I'll take you through. Please follow me."

Max and Gina followed the helpful young lady through the back of the shop front and out into a covered dock area. There was only one boat currently in the dock, by the looks of it an old lobster fishing sloop – the engine compartment was open and there were a couple of people working on the large, half exposed diesel engine.

"Gary, I've got a couple of visitors for you," said the sales assistant.

The larger of the two men working on the motor turned round and looked up at the three people standing on the dock.

"Geez, I've already spent hours telling you guys what I know. I've got a business to run." Gary Stern was clearly annoyed with the interruption.

Max turned to the young woman. "Thanks, we'll take it from here." She got the politely-delivered message to leave and went back to her duties looking after the front of house.

"Mr Stern, my colleague and I only have a few questions and, as we said on the phone this morning, it shouldn't take up much of your valuable time." Gina was firm but insistent in her tone.

"OK. Don, go powder your nose for half an hour," instructed the junior partner in the business. His father was the main driving force behind the operation but since he had contracted cancer, Gary was becoming increasingly the day-to-day boss.

"Sure thing, boss." Don climbed up the ladder onto the dock area and having taken an admiring look at the pretty woman standing next to Max, strode off to go and flirt with the shop assistant.

Gary Stern followed his employee up the ladder and wiped some of the excess engine grease of his hands before extending his hand to Max and Gina in turn.

"Mr. Stern, my name is FBI Agent Bourne." She showed him her badge in case confirmation were required. "And this is Max Thatcher, he's helping us with our enquiries."

Max shook Gary's hand firmly. "Please call me Max."

The men weighed each other up. Gary was only slightly shorter than Max's six foot two frame but shared a similar well-muscled build. Max immediately got the impression this man was ex-services – strange. There was nothing in the briefing note to suggest as much. The man's poise was relaxed but he stood with his feet well spread and his weight on the balls of his feet so that he was well balanced and could move quickly in any direction, offensively or defensively. Not your average boat builder-come-mechanic; of that Max was sure. This guy had definitely done some training.

"A limey, what can I do for you?" The question was asked amicably enough.

"Mr Stern, please could you explain how comes you were in the bay yesterday at that time of morning?" Max's question threw Gina a little; she had expected the line to be to find out what the man had seen.

Max saw the telltale flick away of the man's eyes from his own before the answer came. "As I told you guys last night, I was out collecting pots." From the subconscious body movement Max knew he'd been told a lie; this man was hiding something. The whole of the Boston Harbour area is world renowned for lobster fishing and an untrained eye would not have caught the lie, so for many the answer was totally plausible.

Gina, choosing to forget Max's earlier request, thought she ought to help the man from London out. "Gary ... sorry, do you mind if I call you Gary?" Part of her induction and training process into the FBI had been questioning techniques. Apparently, the best way of getting information was to try and build bonds between the interviewer and interviewee so she went for the first name approach.

"Sure, no problem." Gary gave her a warm smile.

"Great, perhaps you could tell us what you saw yesterday morning?" Max bit his tongue as he could see Gary relax and roll out a well-practised and rehearsed replay of what he saw when the missile struck the airliner. No need to lie; he just told the accurate story of the impact and the subsequent crash into the bay.

He was nearing the end of his narrative. " ... Anyway, I hung around for a little while and reasoned I couldn't do anything to help. I guess I was also in a state of shock so came back here, it was all a bit of a blur." Gary Stern didn't look like a man likely to panic, in Max's opinion, and from what he'd read in the reports Gary had just repeated verbatim the story he had already given; it was almost word perfect. No, from Max's perspective this definitely didn't hang together.

Gina was delighted with how her interview was going; she was getting all the confirmation that she needed that what was in the initial reports was accurate and she was very pleased that she had been able to elicit the same information.

"It must have been very traumatic for you." Gina was close to wrapping up her enquiry and decided that she would have words with Max on the way back to the City about wasting so much time on what was clearly a wild goose chase.

"You've got that right, Agent Bourne, I don't know if I'll ever get over the shock of seeing such a terrible thing." *I bet*, thought Max.

"Anything you'd like to ask, Max?" queried Gina sweetly.

"Only a couple of loose ends to clear up, Gina." He sensed that Gary stiffened again; the man standing opposite was no fool and could see that Max was not as convinced as the pretty FBI agent.

"Really?" Gina had considered that they were done.

"Gary, how many lobster pots were you out emptying last night?" Max saw another lie coming.

"Fifteen or twenty, can't rightly remember. Why?" Gary involuntarily clenched and unclenched his fists; Max didn't miss the sign of stress.

"What were you after? Spiny lobster? I love those big claws," Max asked innocently.

"Yes, managed to get a dozen on board before the business with the plane put an end to the trip." Where was the limey going with this? He didn't like it at all.

Gina had no idea where Max was going with his line of questioning and made an extravagant gesture of looking at her watch. Gary, leapt at the opportunity and looked at his large sports watch too.

"Look, is there anything else I can help you guys with? I've got a lot on, especially with my father not being able to work that much." He was keen to get the interview over with.

Without warning, Max smashed his clenched fist into the man who had brought down the commuter jet just over twenty four hours earlier.

"What the fuck are you doing, Max?" Gina was totally dumbstruck.

Paying her no attention, Max followed up initial strike with another blow to the head and a hard kick to the man's groin. "Stay down if you know what's good for you, pal!"

Gary was lying crumpled on the floor with blood pouring from his mouth and was holding his genital area with both hands as he tried to compute what had just happened. Max's attack had taken him completely off guard; he'd thought the 'interview' all but over and as with the conversation last night with the two local police officers he believed he'd passed easily.

Spitting some blood and a broken tooth out onto the dry dock he looked up at Max in complete shock. "What the fuck are you doing, man? Are you fucking crazy or something?" Gary could see the nothing but menace in Max's eyes, no emotion and no pity.

"Gary," Max crouched down beside the man. "Spiny lobsters don't have big claws, a professional lobster man would know this and that the American Lobsters which do, are out of season. They would also know exactly how many pots they were after for the night and I don't buy for a moment that you would not have stayed and helped to look for survivors. First rule of a seaman, help people out of the water."

"Fuck off, you limey bastard," spat Gary through his broken front teeth.

"Are you crazy Max? Get off him!" Gina didn't know what to do with the man from London; he was clearly a lunatic. This was the second time within twenty four hours that she had seen Max unleash brutal force. She was both in awe of his undoubted capabilities and also frightened at his apparent ability to totally disregard any basic ground rules.

It was as if Gina were not even in the same vicinity . Max pressed on regardless; he knew he had his man and now he needed information, quickly.

"Why did you do it, Gary?" Max had pulled out a wicked looking dive knife and was now standing over the prostrate man. No immediate answer coming forthwith, he kicked the helpless Gary hard in the midriff.

"Max, stop!" Gina had pulled her standard issue pistol out and was pointing it shakily in Max's direction.

Max ignored her entirely and kicked Gary hard in the head. "Gary, I'm going to slice you up. You're not going to prison or through any due process. It's you and me, and either you tell me what I want to know or you are going to suffer pain like you've never experienced."

"Get this mad limey bastard off me," screamed Gary in Gina's direction.

"Max, I'm warning you. I will shoot you!" Gina took the brace position that she had been taught in the academy.

He turned away from Gary. "No you won't, Gina." Max looked at her with dead eyes; he was not for changing.

"Max ..."

Before she had a chance to finish the next lame plea for reason, Max had crossed the distance between them and snatched the gun from her trembling hands. "You can arrest me later, just give me five minutes with this sick bastard." He jammed the gun in the back of his jeans.

"Right Gary, you've got ten seconds to start telling me what I want to know or you're not going to have a life long enough to regret what you've done." He didn't like being rough on Gina, but he was short on time and had little interest in following any rules of normal society - particularly when it came to dealing with a pieces of shit like Gary Stern. He knew he had his man and he was going to get the information he wanted.

Gary was about to repeat telling Max to fuck off, but it had become pretty clear that the man standing over him had little interest in due process. It also occurred to him that the pretty FBI agent weighing in at about one hundred pounds and without her weapon was in no position to stop whatever Max had in mind.

He sat himself up and spat some more blood and another piece of broken tooth out of his mouth.

"If I tell you what I know, what happens to me?" This stopped Gina in her tracks. *Christ*, she thought, as it dawned on her that Max was right.

"You get to walk out of here and Agent Bourne takes you into custody, I imagine you'll cut a deal with the authorities and spend the rest of your life in a cell," replied Max.

"I want more, if I tell you who's behind all the attacks I want to get a better deal." Gary was busy trying to find a way out of his current dilemma on the best terms he could negotiate.

"Gary, I don't have the authority to ..." Max cut Gina off mid flow.

"You lousy piece of shit, right now you should only be concerned with me not cutting you up into little pieces to use for bait in the lobster pots around the bay. What you agree or don't agree with the DA and his team is of little consequence to me, Gary." Max was in no mood to play any sort of cat and mouse game with the terrorist sitting on front of him.

"You're bluffing, I'll do a deal, Agent Bourne, now arrest me," pleaded Gary, having decided that he would be a lot safer in the tender care of the FBI than trying to wriggle his way out his current and all too obviously dangerous predicament.

Max had had enough of being nice. He bent over and dug the dive knife into Gary's right thigh severing neatly, as intended, the femoral artery. Gary let out a scream of pain and placed his hands above the wound which did little to stop his life blood pumping out in time with his racing heart.

"You mother fucka!!!" He couldn't believe what had just happened.

Gina almost passed out at the sight of so much blood.

"Your call Gary, I'll stop the bleeding but only if you tell me now what I want to know." The message was delivered in an even tone.

"All right, there's this woman," Gary said in between gasps of pain.

Max decided to refrain from quipping "there always is ..." but instead contented himself with, "Go on." He sensed the door open behind him as Don came bowling back onto the covered dock. *He must have heard the scream,* thought Max. Seeing his boss lying in an expanding pool of what appeared to be his own blood, and with Max standing over him brandishing a wicked looking blade, he logically assumed that Gary had been attacked by the big man. He looked around for a weapon, settling on a short length of heavy piping he made for Max.

Max had no reason to be overly rough on Don and decided to give him the benefit of doubt and work on the basis that he was not somehow involved in Gary's exploits of the last twenty four hours. As Don approached, he withdrew the pistol from the back of his jeans and pointed it steadily in the new arrival's face.

"Don, I have no quarrel with you. But if you don't back off and drop that pipe right now, you will be a very sorry man. Are we clear?" Don looked at Max and knew instinctively that the threat made was anything but idle. Taking a couple of paces backwards, he dropped the piece of metal.

"Good lad, you know it makes sense." Returning his attention to Gary, Max said, "I reckon you've got 90 seconds before it'll be past mattering and I won't be able to help. For the last time, where is this woman and what's her name?"

Gary was almost delirious with pain and shock. He was the youngest of three boys; his elder brothers had followed in something of a family tradition and gone off to serve in the military; both had served with distinction. John, the eldest, was now working for a large insurance carrier based in Atlanta whilst Matt had cut himself out a good career working in Chicago as an analyst for a commodities broker. Gary, in most people's vernacular, was a bit of a 'fuck up'; he hadn't done well at school and had flunked out of college after a couple of terms. He wasn't particularly stupid, he just had a natural talent for getting in with the wrong crowd and being easily led.

His constant run-ins with the local police force and his poor educational record made him basically unemployable. The head of the family, a hardworking and god fearing man, almost begrudgingly gave him a job in the boat business. The father had hoped to pass on the business to one of his sons; it would be fair to say the Gary would not have been his first choice and he made little secret of the fact. Gary hated his work, despised his father with his holier-than-thou morals and was extremely envious of his older brothers' successes. He was pliable and weak; easy to manipulate and a natural candidate for Control.

"I met her in North Africa just over a year ago; she was in this training camp that I had gone to. They teach you how to blow things up, to shoot properly and fill your head with crap about freedom from persecution by the imperialist states. Come on Max, for Christ's sake I'm bleeding out here man ..." He had fallen for the sexy Control in an instant; she made him feel special and convinced him that he was a man capable of great things. His latent rage and frustration were all too obvious for someone like Control to spot; the fool didn't need a cause, he just wanted to be famous and the centre of attention.

"Yep looks that way, so I wouldn't waste your breath." Max was in no mood for pity. He'd lost that element in his personal make up when he had watched the bomb go off on Madeira. Whether Gary lived or died was of little consequence in his mind, all he cared about was stamping out the organisation behind the bombings.

Don and Gina looked on, transfixed, as Gary continued. "Anyway, I had only gone there because I was bored of life here and wanted some adventure. Running around the African bush and becoming a sometime mercenary appealed. This woman showed me how fucked up we are in the States and convinced me that I ought to strike at the heart of the sick and soft country that we had become." Lying on his father's dock and rapidly bleeding to death hadn't been part of the plan. He'd never truly suffered pain of any description, and the realities of blowing up innocent people on a jet liner had escaped his sick warped mind entirely. When he had pulled the trigger it was like playing a video game, and when the plane had blown up he hadn't thought twice about what he had done; it all seemed somehow remote and detached from real life.

"Why on earth would you want to bring down an airliner?" Gina was appalled and couldn't help herself but ask the question.

"To prove how easy it was." Gary then reverted to the message that he had been sold. "To show that we Americans are not invincible and that because of all the things we do around the world, and meddling in other people's affairs, we the great American population are fair targets." The blood was continuing to pump between his hands and Max could see that Gary was visibly fading. "Because of what I've done, millions of Americans will now take more interest in what we do around the globe and the security services will work that much harder to make sure that it's not so easy to carry out a bombing." He was beginning to convince himself all over again that he was in fact a freedom fighter for justice, a hero and not just a coward who had pulled a trigger and run away.

"Are you fucking nuts? Are you trying to tell me that what you've done is good for the country?" Gina was incandescently angry and frankly couldn't believe the rubbish coming out of the mouth of the man who was bleeding to death in front of her. From the safe and warm seat in her office she had little, if any, exposure to the crazy people who were out there roaming free in the big bad world. She had read about these deluded and dangerous individuals, but seeing one up close and personal brought the realities of what she and her colleagues did very much into focus.

Max could see from her body language and tone of voice that today's experience would change Gina's view of life and her work forever. *Probably not what she expected when she got out of bed this morning,* he mused.

"Give me her name, Gary, the location of where this woman is now, and the training camp details." Max wasn't interested in a deluded man's reasoning for blowing up a plane full of innocent commuters. There was not and never would be any justification for this wanton act of murder. He'd dealt with enough lunatics over time to know that they would try and convince themselves that they served some higher purpose and that they were not governed by the normal rules of society.

A trained soldier, Max had seen too much death in his time. He took no pleasure in killing or inflicting pain but had understood from the outset that this was something that he might have to do in his career. He had, however, normally engaged with other combatants who knew and, for the most part, respected the rules. It was totally abhorrent to him, and to any sane person for that matter, that one would simply snuff out so many innocent lives simply because one could. Terrorists chose weak, soft targets; they were cowards of the first order in his book.

Gary was continuing his pathetic story. "I don't know her real name, everyone in the camp in Somalia goes by a made up name given to them when they arrive. She wasn't a proper terrorist like the rest of us, she was a reporter. Please help, I'm dying."

"How do you make contact with her now?" Ignoring the bomber's plea - as far as he was concerned, he would happily let the man bleed to death - Max pressed on.

"Via email and the odd phone call – please, I'm begging you, I don't know where she is; she's got your accent though. I don't know her as anything other than Control." Gary was in tears by now, the pain and the fear of death working their magic on this broken pathetic man now totally bereft of his former self confidence.

Max wasn't surprised at the response. "What do you know about the other bombers?"

Gary would tell Max anything he knew; he didn't want to die. He'd never been knifed and the pain was nothing like he had ever experienced. The blood kept pumping through his fingers and he was becoming light headed; this was not like a video game and he was terribly frightened. "Nothing, you have to believe me. I was shocked at the news, I thought I was the only one in her circle."

Max looked across at Gina and nodded, he had what he believed he could get for now. "Don, go call 911 – get the ambulance and some police out here right now," instructed the FBI agent.

Max bent down to the stricken man and pulled the belt from his blood soaked jeans; he wrapped the belt around the upper thigh and yanked it tight. This elicited another scream of pain from Gary but at the same time cut the flow of leaking blood from the knife wound to a trickle.

"If I had my way, I'd push you over the side of the dock and let you drown, you sick bastard," said Max; his voice was audibly carrying a degree of remorse that he couldn't carry out his preference and despatch Gary to a watery grave. Gary was left under no illusion that the man from the UK meant every word. Max turned on his heel and walked back through the shop, past the dazed shop assistant and out to the parked Mercedes.

Leaving Don, who had returned from calling the local police and ambulance, with clear instructions not to let the man out of his sight, Gina followed him out to her car. "How did you know?"

Max turned and faced her across the roof of the Mercedes, his hard eyes portraying just a hint of wicked devil may care mirth. "I didn't for sure, but I had enough of a hunch that it was worth potentially getting told off by you for throwing the first punch."

They could hear the faint sound of a siren approaching; Max somehow doubted that the man lying on the floor of the dock yard was going to get terribly sympathetic treatment from either the police or ambulance crew. Max opened the passenger door and climbed into his seat and started working on his iPhone; he had to get a report off to London and let Patrick know what he had found out.

Gina waited outside the car for the arriving Boston police; once they had arrived she gave them a rapid briefing, making it clear that the ambulance was to take the suspect to the military hospital at the nearby naval base. Satisfied that her instructions were crystal clear she followed Max's lead, climbed in next to him and started up the Autobahn express. "Jesus, are you for real? Where to now?"

"The airport."

Paris – Tuesday, Early Afternoon

The two Falcon Services operatives were sitting in the head of the DRM's expansive office overlooking the Champs Elysees. Apparently the smoking ban on public places didn't extend to government offices, and Gerard was able to keep up his sixty-a-day habit without having to brave the French pavements.

Francois and Greg had spent a fairly fruitless morning looking around the scene of the Metro bombing. They had been allowed down into the tunnel to see for themselves the terrible damage done. In such an enclosed space, the full impact of the bomb had been felt down the entire length of the train. For both operatives it was a bit of a mystery as to how all the twisted wreckage was going to be removed. It was almost impossible to get heavy lifting equipment down to where the stricken metro carriages lay on their side in a tangled mess. There seemed little alternative but to painstakingly cut the metal into manageable pieces so that they could be dragged down the tunnel and lifted onto waiting flat carriages.

They were left in no doubt that it would take a long time. The floodlit onsite investigators were still going through the ruined metal and undertaking the awful task of removing body parts as they went. In short, it was horrific, and would have turned the stomachs of less experienced people.

It was a complete mystery to Greg what would drive people to doing such a dreadful thing, and he said as much to Francois on the short taxi ride over to meet with the head of the DRM.

"Greg, the world is full of disenfranchised individuals and unfortunately some of them become so desperate they do things like you've seen this morning." Francois had spent many years serving in North Africa and had witnessed, any number of times, the awful conditions that people lived in. In Africa, life was considered cheap and he had seen the terrible inter-tribal violence that erupted on a regular basis.

The younger man had seen his own fair share of action and visited places that would not make it any time soon on to a holiday programme. "I get that, Francois, but it's the complete randomness that I don't follow. There is no science to blowing up a packed train on the Metro. You have no idea who you are going to kill or maim; for all you know some of the people might even be supporters of whatever the cause was in the first place."

"You are, of course, correct, my friend, but you forget one thing," replied Francois.

"And that is?" queried Greg.

"You are not a terrorist, you live by the rules that society have defined. Thus, my friend, your whole value system is completely different; you see a person on a train, a terrorist simply sees nothing but a means of delivering a message. Whereas you see individuals with families and normal lives, a bomber sees an opportunity to spread fear and chaos." Francois took a brief pause and looked out of the window at his beloved Paris. "These bastards don't care about life, least of all their own. They do not want to conform to our way of life, they want to undermine and destroy it."

"Where do you draw the line, Francois? What happens if you've tried to tell your message and no one wants to listen?" Greg totally agreed with the points his colleague and friend had made, but he could also see another side of the argument. After all, the British and French had in their long history also done some terrible things around the world as they had grown their respective empires.

The taxi pulled up outside an imposing old building. "Ah, mon ami, that is the eternal question. 'One man's ...'" he didn't bother to finish the well-known saying as he got out of the car.

The two Falcon Service operatives climbed the impressive stone entrance stairs that led them to the heart of the DRM. Having passed through stringent security measures, they made themselves known to the receptionist. A few minutes later they were met by a very shapely secretary who led them via the elevator to the head of the DRM's fourth floor corner office.

The men all knew one another, and once they had caught up with each other's domestic developments they got down to the business of the day.

Greg tabled the question. "Gerard, what do you think happened in the tunnel? Was is it a 'timed' bomb or did someone blow themselves up along with everybody else?" It had been agreed that the discussion would be held in English, as Greg's French simply wasn't good enough for the topics that needed to be explored.

"We're not sure, to be honest," Gerard's English was impeccable. He had spent many years working across the globe and whilst he was a very proud Frenchman, he had come very quickly to accept the necessity of speaking good English. "Until the forensic guys put the device back together and establish whether there was a timing device, we can't be one hundred per cent confident either way."

Francois went to the window and looked down the Champs Elysees, the world famous road with the Place de La Concorde at one end and the Arc De Triomphe at the other. He never tired of the sight, and would always make the point, whenever possible, to take a long walk along the road. He thoroughly enjoyed stopping for a while to watch the free entertainment at the Arc De Triomphe as drivers did their best to navigate possibly the largest roundabout in the world.

His ex-wife also used to like to take the stroll to enjoy a bit of window shopping in the fabulously expensive boutiques. They had amicably split a couple of years ago; there being no children involved they had simply decided to pursue their lives in different directions. Francois regretted the divorce in some ways but had rationalised that Giselle, his now ex-wife, would be far happier with a husband who spent more time at home. He had served in the forces all his life and recognised that he wasn't devoting as much time as he should to his wife. An extremely good looking woman, it hadn't taken long for her to find a rich banker who was now keeping her in some style. By all accounts, she no longer only window shopped but rather went in and bought whatever took her fancy. He was happy for her; for his part, he had a string of girlfriends, some of whom weren't even married.

Francois returned his full attention to the meeting. "Sounds to me as though we really still have no starting point. Has there been any sensible 'claim' for the bombing?" He said this although how one could have any pride in claiming culpability for the slaughter of so many innocents was totally beyond his powers of reasoning.

"Non, nothing. It's almost as though the odd small device in a parked car is one thing; whilst letting off explosives in a packed commuter train is beyond the pale even for hardened terrorists. Interestingly, even the praises for the outrage have been somewhat muted compared to what we might have expected." Gerard stubbed out his Gauloises and in the same motion reached for another, which he lit with a deft skill that he had developed over many years to ensure his lungs were never contaminated with fresh air.

"As you know, Paris has received at least its fair share of terrorist threats over the years, which has for example resulted in the Eiffel Tower being closed on a number of occasions. In addition, the odd flight has been cancelled due to fears of a bombing, but thankfully nothing on the scale of yesterday's outrage had so far happened." He paused to take a long puff on his cigarette. Exhaling slowly, Gerard continued, "France has an active foreign policy and we have made a number of enemies around the globe, not only for our direct engagements but also through the direct and indirect support that we have lent to the USA or UK." It was an unfortunate fact of life that France was a known target; Gerard held himself personally responsible and was racked with guilt that he had failed to prevent the tube bombing.

"How are the investigations going?" enquired Francois.

"We are reviewing all the CCTV footage that we have, and of course shaking all the trees we can think of to try and find these animals. We will find them, of this I have no doubt." Gerard's tone making it abundantly clear that he was totally confident in his ability to bring the terrorist to justice.

Greg felt his mobile phone vibrate in his pocket, indicating that had received a message. "Excuse me, looks like I need to call the office." He left the two men in the smoke-filled office and went off in search of a quiet corner where he wouldn't be interrupted or overheard so that he could talk freely to Patrick in London.

Fifteen minutes later, he had fully briefed Francois and Gerard on the results of Max's somewhat unorthodox interviewing techniques. He could imagine that, despite the Boston bomber's admission of guilt in front of witnesses, that some civil rights lawyer was going to try and make a name for themselves by having a pop at how Max managed to secure the much-needed information. He doubted very much that Max could care less, and correctly judged that he would leave that inconvenient problem with the Americans to resolve.

"Well, I guess the focus needs to be to find this woman called 'Control'," ventured Francois. "Any ideas how we narrow down the search?"

Gerard thought about this for a couple of moments. "We've got some resources undercover working in Somalia. I will put some calls in and see if we can shed any light on this woman's identity."

Francois had seen active service in the part of the world. "The problem is it's like a sieve, it's far too easy for people to come and go. It's not unusual for them to let in TV crews, it's 'shock TV' in my opinion and free publicity to the wrong sort of people. Can't remember which company was involved but al-Shabaab is one of the camps that's made its way regularly into the news."

"Yep, I heard about that," confirmed Greg. "Didn't the Kenyans bomb it recently?"

"Yes. Apparently they didn't take very kindly to one of their shopping malls getting all shot up, and they had a pretty good idea where the problem originated from." Gerard had seen the reports and was also cognisant of the fact that the French intelligence services had helped compile the evidence.

It was agreed that they would touch base later that evening to update one another on any progress made. Gerard kindly organised a car to take Greg and Francois back to the Eurostar terminus for their two hour trip back to London.

From the call with Patrick Greg had established that Max was due back in London later that night and it had been agreed that the team would reconvene with supplemental members augmented from Admiral Walker's inner sanctum. Settling into his first class seat Greg shut his eyes and tried to sleep through the high speed rail journey back to London. It was, he mused, most likely going to be a long night.

News 24 Studios, South Bank – Tuesday, Evening

Jo, also known as Control, had devised a well-crafted plan to make sure that she not only delivered an unforgettable message to the populations of the UK, France and the USA but also that the family name of Lockton would never be forgotten; something which she knew was most close to her father's heart. What, of course, wouldn't have given him any satisfaction, though from her warped perspective was almost the best part, was that she would be ensuring that it would be a name written down and immortalised in the history books for all the wrong reasons.

She was sat at her desk in the low-slung building overlooking the Thames. From the outside the TV studio, with its windowless facade, looked more like a bomb shelter than a place of work. Some 1980s architect had convinced the planners that a lump of sharp-edged concrete would look good plonked on the banks of the river. The location may have been excellent for those wishing to work in the centre of London, but the lack of any natural daylight created a surreal - some would say claustrophobic - atmosphere inside the building. Time didn't have any meaning, other than being a series of numbers displayed on the multitude of digital clocks dotted around the building.

Apparently, the concept was to create a timeless piece of architecture both from the outside and internally. There was no day or night, so the only way one knew if it was raining or if the sun was shining was when one left the building to get away from the air conditioning or watched a live outside broadcast. Most of the people who worked there hated the building, but it was the London home to probably the most influential news channel in the world. The owners liked to convince themselves that, as they were responsible for delivering the news 24 hours a day, seven days a week, it made little difference whether the sun or moon could be seen by those working from within their London location.

The building divided itself across three floors above ground with a large basement area that housed the IT and telecommunications equipment. The top expanse of office space was set aside for meeting rooms and open plan seating for the myriad reporters and the administrative support teams that supported the day-to-day operation of the site. The first floor had a void in the middle and was allocated for the numerous TV studios and senior executive offices. Each of the dozen or so rooms backed on to the atrium, so that one could see through the soundproofed glass at the back of the studios or offices down on to the ground floor and the heart of the building: the newsroom.

The newsroom was a hive of activity almost 24 hours a day with field reporters and journalists meeting with the various programme editors to work through the material coming in from around the world. The space was about half the size of a soccer pitch, teemed with life and had a constant buzz. Around the edges of the room, there was any number of television monitors silently replaying either home produced work or keeping a wary eye on what the competition was churning out.

Everything had been going along nicely according to Jo's plan; that was, until she had seen the message coming in over the news feeds that a suspect for the Boston atrocity had been arrested. That wasn't supposed to have happened, not yet at any rate. She logged on to her computer and started scanning through various social media sites. No name had been released officially but she was pretty sure that the power of the Internet to spread confidential information at the press of a few key strokes wouldn't disappoint.

It only took ten minutes of hunting and she had found what she was looking for. She rather hoped they had the wrong person. But there, in one of the many conspiracy-focused chat rooms, she read the name of Gary Stern. Under the auspices of protecting the public's rights to freedom of speech and access to information, these sites prided themselves on releasing information which government agencies would otherwise like to keep quiet about. Not only did this often cause embarrassment to those in power who might be wishing to keep something out of the public gaze, but it also meant that those less scrupulous members of society would be tipped off.

Over the past couple of years there had been a lot of public outrage, in large parts stoked by the press, about how the various arms of any number of sovereign nations' secret services had been spying on the normal citizen. The various highly questionable exploits of the now deceased Jack Hunter and his Gatekeeper software had simply served to illustrate how easy it was for less than scrupulous individuals to steal both corporate and private information from anyone using a computer system. To compound matters, the whole world relied on computers, ipso facto it meant that anybody with sufficient resources would be well capable of repeating what he had done.

The Snowden revelations about the level of intelligence gathering undertaken by the CIA, NSA and various other American governmental bodies resulted in him being labelled as a hero by some and traitors by others. Jo was only too aware that the outcry in the 'free' press about data privacy was also somewhat self-serving. There had been several instances where the press had used the very same techniques that were 'so insidious', by all accounts, to gather information to assist in getting exclusives on members of the glitterazzi, or in pursuit of a scoop that might involve at the time relatively unknown members of the general public.

In any event, Jo was very well versed in how to source information; you just needed to know where to look and Jo was very proficient in this regard.

From what she could ascertain, the suspect was under police guard at a military hospital on the outskirts of the city. She concluded that this would be as much for his own protection as any particular security issues. Feelings would be running very high in Boston and she could easily imagine the man being lynched from the nearest stop light if the masses got their way.

Control was disappointed with the news but had already factored something of this nature into her thinking. She had been, and indeed still was, a first rate chess player. She had filled countless hours of unloved time spent on her own whilst in the stately home with logic puzzles and solving cryptic conundrums. Jo had read innumerable books about the game of chess and had over the years played against a host of imaginary opponents on the small computer chess board game that she had once received as a Christmas present. She loved the strategy, the multi-dimensional nature of the game and the ruthlessness of the great masters whom she had studied at such great length.

The main element of her game plan was yet to come to life; the pieces were all on the board and the opening gambit had played out as expected. Now, in the middle part of the game, she had to make sure that her overall strategy wasn't derailed before the final end game could be played out.

Picking up her coat to keep out the early evening chill, she left the TV studios and crossed the Thames via the Millennium Bridge; loving referred to, at least initially, by the local London population as the wibbly wobbly bridge. It had earned this moniker due to its ability to make people sea sick as they crossed the river because of a now-rectified design flaw. It had been a PR disaster of epic proportions and a source of great amusement for those not to have been tainted by the project.

The weather had turned and was bitter; whilst the temperature was above zero degrees, the piercing wind carried a dampness with it that cut to the bone. She lit another cigarette, pulled her coat tight around her good looking body and made the climb up the stairs to the iconic Cathedral that stands majestically upon the brow of hill looking out across the river. Walking in the shadow of St Paul's, she bought four disposable SIM cards from four different shops; this was to make sure that she left no lasting impression in the mind of any of the shop assistants. She then sent four short messages, each one sent using one of the individually purchased phone cards. Satisfied, she returned the way she had come only stopping briefly to deposit the phone and cards in the Thames for safe keeping. Enjoying another smoke, she passed only a few people as she made her way back to the bunker on the Thames to present the forthcoming security slot on the extended news bulletin.

She had deployed her pawns; they were out on the board. She had no loyalty for the people that she had turned and persuaded to do the terrible things that they had done. Her foot soldiers were there to be sacrificed as required to protect the capital pieces which were needed to support her overall strategy.

Chiswick – Tuesday, 23.00

Max had made the trip back to London in good time on a private jet which had been chartered at the behest of Admiral Walker. He'd been in his office building for about an hour and was glad that he had managed to grab a couple of hours' sleep on the flight over. Gina, with some encouragement from her superiors, had very much wanted to make the trip back with Max. In truth she had come to the conclusion that life was never likely to be dull hanging around Max, and she had more confidence in his ability to make material progress quickly than the multitude of agents still looking for a starting point. She also had more personal reasons for wanting to make the trip, but those would have to wait for the next time they met, hopefully in a less stressful environment.

Max had discussed with Gina at length the prospect of her coming to the UK, and had finally persuaded her that she could probably do more good remaining in the USA and updating her people on what Mr Stern had had to say for himself. Max liked Gina; she had been most helpful during his short stay in the US. The harsh reality from his perspective was that, had she made the trip to the UK, she would have added minimal or any material benefit to the process; at least that's what he tried to convince himself. In truth he could see their relationship perhaps becoming more complex and developing into more than simply work.

As Max had predicted and subsequently confirmed in a brief note from Gina, once the delusional Gary had got to hospital he had been formally cautioned and then due process had taken over so that he was now sheltering behind the long arm of civil rights. His court-appointed lawyer had made it abundantly clear that his client had nothing to say and that anything that had been beaten out of him wouldn't stand up in a court of law.

 For all intents and purposes the US Government was no further forward in its 'official' investigations. They would have to be patient and, in the absence of any hard evidence, try to coax a formal confession out of the man that they knew to be guilty. In all probability this would have to be achieved in the less than satisfactory old 'plea bargaining' way. Steve Brewer, now full briefed, was however extremely grateful to the Admiral for providing a more direct means of extracting information and had conveyed as much in a call earlier that evening.

~

"You're very welcome, Steve." Admiral Walker was pleased to receive the thanks but even happier that his decision to involve Max directly had reaped dividends so quickly.

"I'm sure glad he's one of the good guys, Gordon. From what I got from our field agent, he takes no prisoners and was pretty brutal with the guy." It would never have occurred to the Director to follow up a few good punches and kicks with the use of dive knife rather than the threat of a gun. He appreciated that the use of the knife was that much more personal and, of course, could be used in the hands of a professional without the risk of killing the man. No, on balance, he concluded that he'd have gone with the waving–the-gun-around routine and probably as a result achieved far less. Then again, he mused, as Director of the FBI he was basically a desk jockey and pretty far removed from what happened in the field.

Max's long-time friend and former commanding officer couldn't help but let out a little chuckle. "You don't want to be on the wrong side of Max, that's for sure. I will try and give you a call in few hours to catch up on progress. OK?"

"Sure thing, speak later." Steve replaced the phone in its cradle and went back to studying a list of Gary Stern's known associates. Pretty short list; the guy was obviously something of a loner. He would check in with Gina's boss a little later in the day to see if there were any useful details coming out of the research. Somehow he doubted the names would be any more than dead ends, but he couldn't afford to take the chance.

~

The Falcon Services meeting room in West London was fairly full by the time everyone had taken their seats. The group had convened here as much as anything for a change of scenery; there had been no news through official channels for several hours. The attendees travelling down from their offices a few miles to the east were happy to have the break and it also meant that, as Max had arrived into Heathrow, he wouldn't have to cross town in order to deliver his briefing. Those present included the heads of both MI5 and MI6, Admiral Walker, Greg, Patrick, Pete and an agitated Max who was pacing up and down the room.

"What the hell do you mean it's public domain that the Americans have arrested that deluded psycho Gary Stern? I made it abundantly clear that we wanted to keep that information quiet. Who the hell let the cat out of the bag?" He was livid.

"I'm afraid it's not that simple, Max. I found out from the Internet within an hour of when you and I spoke," answered Patrick. "The problem is that you've got all these people who believe in freedom of speech. Feelings are obviously running high, and the American public are baying for blood."

"Whatever ..." Max was clearly annoyed. He understood better than most that whoever Control was would now also know that the various agencies looking for her had got a break. So in all probability, this would mean that she would want to make sure she covered her tracks even more deeply.

"How's the narrowing down process going for our potential suspects?" asked Admiral Walker.

"We've been going through our files at MI5 and MI6, Admiral, and have a list of some two hundred profiles which might meet the criteria of English/Female/Reporter/Somalia training camps," Charlie Marsh responded on his and Jessica Brown's, the head of MI6's, behalf.

"Any favourites?" enquired Greg.

"No clear ones," conceded the head of MI5.

The Admiral stretched his arms above his head and couldn't help prevent a huge yawn. "Sorry ... well, at least we have a starting point and that's better than where we were a few hours ago."

"Are we sure that Gary was telling the truth?" asked Jessica. "He could have made it up for all we know."

"It's a fair concern," conceded Max. "He seemed pretty sincere when he told me."

"Jessica, I don't know if you already know this but Max used more than his charming personality to get the information out of our Mr Stern."

"No, I didn't, Admiral," she replied. "Presumably that would explain why the man is in hospital and not a high security holding area. OK, I'll buy the information is valid, at least as far as Gary was concerned."

"What else have we got?" Max wanted to move on.

"I'm intrigued, as I'm sure we all are, by the text message that was sent to Scotland Yard less than a couple of hours ago," said Pete. "Any idea what it means, Patrick?"

"Are we sure it has anything to do with this investigation?" asked the Admiral. It occurred to the assembled group that it would be an easy matter for their investigations to be sent off up a blind alley by some hoaxer sending spurious information through. There was no shortage of data being crunched in London, Paris or Washington. The trick was being able to determine what was real and what was simply chaff.

Patrick considered for a moment. "Not sure, in truth, Admiral. I've been giving it a lot of thought. In the absence of any other leads I'm tempted to assume that the message is relevant. If it's valid then I would assume that it's clearly trying to point us in a direction." He wasn't happy without confirmation that the information was pertinent, to commit time and resources to investigating it further, but so far they had little else to work with. "Any objections to spending a bit of time trying to work out the significance, if any, of the message?" There being none, he flicked a button on the projector sitting on the meeting room table; the image displayed was bright enough to read without the need to dim the room lights. He read it aloud:

"A tenth of a pointless march executed in three locations plus a French supermini meets an abundant fishing place at the white Kings home"

"Incidentally, it would appear that similar cryptic clues have been sent to Paris and Washington within the last couple of hours. This adds credence to the theory that they relate to the bombings, but of course we don't know if they are from this 'Control' woman. But we do know they were all sent from London," Charlie volunteered.

"Hopefully they're quicker than we are at solving the riddle," added the head of MI5.

"I think may have some of it," offered Jessica. She walked to the whiteboard where the image was displaying. She picked up a dry board marker pen and did a quick check to make sure it wasn't for flip charts. Satisfied, she said, "Look," and began marking the board.

"A //tenth of a pointless march executed in three locations// plus a French supermini// meets an abundant fishing place// at the white Kings home"

"It's been nagging away at me for the last hour or so. The only pointless march I can think of that we'd all know about is the Duke of York and his 10,000 men that marched up and down the hill. A tenth would be 1,000 and then do it three times equals 3,000."

"Go on," encouraged Patrick. It never ceased to amaze him that by putting something up on the whiteboard in public gaze how much more input one received than simply sending around a note asking for help. Clearly one idea set off another and the fact that Jessica had simply drawn a few vertical lines had clearly switched the lights on in numerous brains around the table.

Jessica wrote 3,000 on the board. "French supermini," she read out loud. "I'm sure I've heard that expression ..."

"Maybe it's something to do with miniskirts or fashion?" offered Greg.

"Wishful thinking I reckon, mate," commented Patrick.

"A French supermini is a Peugeot 205," interjected Francois.

"That's it. Quite right Francois, I used to own a bright red one when I was at college," confessed Jessica.

"So if we add the 'A' back now we have," she wrote as she spoke, "A3205? A road or grid reference maybe?"

Pete had been tapping away on his laptop. "It's a road just on the south side of the river by Wandsworth Bridge, just around the corner from Clapham Junction." He pulled up the map on full screen and placed it on the meeting room table so that everyone could crowd round and have a look at it.

They were all mentally exhausted. None of the people in the room apparently could do much with the next part of the puzzle and all sat staring rather aimlessly at the clue on the screen.

"How stupid am I?" Max stood up and pointed to Usk Road on the enlarged map on Pete's laptop. "Sorry guys, should have seen the connection earlier; the river Usk, and there are a few of them get their names from old Celtic – it means *a place full of abundant fish*." He'd seen the reference before in several of the salmon fishing books that he liked to pick up from time to time, fly fishing being one of his favourite pastimes when could find the time.

"Which leaves us with *the white Kings home*," said Greg; he decide his forte might lie in reading the clues as opposed to trying to solve them.

As one Patrick and Jessica said, "E1." There were blank stares around the room. "It's where the white king starts on a chess board," explained Jessica.

"So what have we got A3205, York Road which as it happens conveniently confirms the marching connection, Usk Road, a flat or apartment E1." Patrick read out the 'solved' conundrum.

"Well it's an answer, heaven knows if it's the right one," said Admiral Walker.

Max picked up his jacket "Well, let's go find out. Francois, Greg, with me, please."

Marylebone, London - Tuesday, 23.30

The three of them had met up for drinks as planned earlier in the evening following Jo's final performance of the day on News 24. She had become even more of a celebrity during the last twenty four hours, as viewers outraged by the bombings had tuned in hungry for more information about the terrorists responsible. Every taxi journey was now accompanied by the, "'Hey, aren't you that Jo Lockton off the TV ...?" She confessed to herself that she was rather enjoying being in the limelight.

The private club off Berkeley Square in the West End was full as usual. Most of the well-heeled customers who frequented it lived in central London; so the inconvenience of the odd bomb going off at a main line commuter station rather passed them by. Jo suspected that, in truth, many of the revellers wouldn't know a packed commuter train unless it landed on them. Nasty things like terrorists bombs happened to the 'other' poor people that they sometimes passed on a shopping trip. Drugs, booze and generally having a good time was all that consumed their otherwise empty lives.

The music was loud and the prices of the drinks were extortionate. Still, if you could afford the annual invite-only membership and therefore were most likely not on the breadline, who cared? Most of the occupants didn't have an early morning call to worry about so one could reliably party on into the wee hours most mornings.

A couple of sharp mojitos had helped keep Jo suitably pumped full of adrenalin. Doing live TV was a rush in its own right, but now that she was so regularly the focal point of the extended specials, and with her own plan coming to a head she was on a real high. Tomorrow's one hour long special would be the pinnacle of her career, and she was wired.

She wanted more than a few drinks and the odd dance to celebrate and, as hoped, she had little problem encouraging her drinking partners to accompany her home to share a far more intimate evening.

The three of them had shared a black cab back to Control's apartment. The very expensive accommodation was in the heart of Marylebone in a small mews. The highly fashionable and much sought after residential area of Marylebone has all the qualities of being almost its own private village or enclave, despite being set within the very heart of central London. Less than a mile square, one could easily believe that Marylebone was set in the leafy suburbs and not on the West End's busy doorstep, or a mile and a bit from the largest financial centre in the world. In keeping with her tastes, the two bedroom flat was very minimalist in its décor; she led her guests off the main hall and into the master bedroom suite and stripped.

Jo rolled onto her side and pressed her naked body against Petra, a gorgeous Russian exotic dancer whom she had met a couple of months ago when she'd been out for a night with the boys from the office. She ran her hands all over her beautifully toned and taut skin; perhaps she ought to start working out in the night clubs dancing for a living instead of the expensive gym she was a member of?

She felt Alex's aroused penis pressed up against her back side as he gently used his left hand to play with her clitoris; she was becoming hugely excited and could feel her wetness running down onto his well-practised fingers. Jo moved backwards a little, feeling Alex's cock start to edge into her anal region, *maybe later,* she thought, but for now she wanted to concentrate on Petra.

Having created a little space, she got Petra to lie on her back and climbed on top of her; Alex sat on the edge of the bed playing with himself and watched Jo as she climbed on top of the exotic dancer and rubbed her vaginal region hard against Petra shaven area. She pinned the younger woman's arms behind her head and extracted a strap on sex toy from the conveniently placed beside cabinet. She tightened the belt around herself and drove the artificial stimulant into Petra. She lay across the dancer and drove her hips forward as though she were a man fucking the blonde lying beneath her. Petra responded by wrapping her legs around Jo's back pulling her in more deeply. Alex stood by the side of the bed and watched as the two women wound themselves ever tighter into each other embrace. Jo gently pushed Petra away from her and kissed Petra hard on the lips before continuing her journey south via the pert hard nipples which she took in turn and sucked them until the dancer gave out a little cry of half-felt pain.

She used her hands to spread the woman beneath her legs a little further and opened the lips of her labia so she could bury her face fully and enjoy the taste of her highly aroused partner for the evening. This was all too much for Alex to watch and not become involved; he moved around the bed and lifted Jo's hips none too gently so that he could position himself behind her whilst she serviced Petra.

The effect on three of them was electric. Alex took his engorged manhood and positioned it so that he could slide it easily into Jo's soaking vagina. Jo was close to orgasm, the now once again writhing Petra was using her hands to force Jo's face and mouth ever deeper into her – the smell, the taste and a rock hard cock fucking her hard and roughly from behind combined to bring Jo to a shuddering and noisy conclusion.

She felt Alex explode and as he slowly withered within her, Petra - who must have sensed the man's ejaculation – climaxed, shooting warm fluid all over Jo's face. Jo rolled over onto her back and looked at the mirror on the ceiling; that was great, what a fabulous end to a most productive couple of days.

The three of them collapsed exhausted and caressed each other into a light doze.

Paris – Wednesday, 01.25

Truth be told, the French had solved their riddle the quickest of the three teams and already staked out an apartment in the eighteenth arrondissement: Montmartre, a favourite tourist quarter of the city. Famed for its small squares and ever-present street artists, with Sacre Coeur perched on top of the hill commanding fabulous views over the rest of Paris. It was dark and the elite RAID (Recherche Assistance Intervention Dissuasion) police team unsurprisingly had little interest in the tourist attractions that may or not be on offer.

The street lights for that block had been switched off at the central power station, and there were no people to be seen walking around at that time of night. To be sure that there were no unwelcome civilian casualties, the police had thrown a four hundred metre cordon around the target building. For the past thirty minutes the adjacent buildings had been quietly evacuated. Ideally they would have emptied the building that they were proposing to go in to but had considered that this would not be practical without alerting the suspects.

It was cold and wet; the breath of the waiting men all dressed in black and wearing balaclavas could be seen condensing in what little ambient light leaked from neighbouring streets, making it look as though there were a group of people standing around having a smoke outside of a bar.

The order was given for the two squads, each comprising eight men, to go into the building. Wearing full Kevlar body armour under their black outer garb, the heavily armed teams separated, one taking the elevator in two runs to the top floor where it was then disabled. The other group made the climb to the sixth floor via the wooden staircase which snaked itself up the inside of the old building. Snipers had been positioned opposite the building to ensure that no one tried to make an escape by climbing down the outside of the building using the less than secure looking fire escape.

"Alpha 1 in position." This fire team had made its way down from the eighth floor, the top of the building, and were now positioned along the corridor outside the target apartment on the sixth floor. Their job would be to go into the flat and take out whomever was there. The expectation was that they were dealing with vicious terrorists, so the taking of prisoners, whilst a bonus, was not an overriding priority for the mission.

"Delta 1 in position." The backup team was now spaced out along the staircase.

"Allez, allez!" came the command through the headphones. The lead Special Forces police officer crashed through the door into the apartment. He moved down the corridor and came to the first room of the apartment. What he saw stopped him dead in his tracks; he was followed in by his colleagues with their guns at the ready. There was a television with its volume control set on high in the corner of what appeared to be the main living area. A young boy of about twelve was staring intently at the screen, his throat had been cut and had it not fallen backwards against the blood-soaked chair, his head would most likely have come off completely. Even for a hardened professional, the scene almost made the lead officer gag.

The team spread out through the apartment looking for more occupants in other parts of the large accommodation. As they left the lounge behind them and moved further into the three bedroom flat, they could hear a man's voice apparently pleading with another person in the room from behind the door that they now stood outside.

The words were hard to discern but sounded like Darija, modern Arabic, to the fire team leader. He'd been to Morocco on several occasions but his mastery of the language was not good enough to understand what was being said. He indicated to his number two to kick the wooden door down. The door splintered from the solid strike and the two men entered the main bedroom with their weapons at the ready to see a man on his knees; hands clasped in front of him. He was only wearing what looked like the bottom of black pyjama set.

Standing in front of him was a woman wearing not much more than a closely packed explosives vest as worn by suicide bombers. She held a bloodied blade in her right hand and had a complete look of shock as the two men from RAID had burst into the room. The pair had been so engrossed in their heated discussions that they obviously hadn't heard the front door give way over the noise of the TV set still blaring down the hall.

For a split second, there was silence, and nobody moved. Alpha team leader made a snap decision and shot the woman through the centre of her forehead; she fell backward leaving remnants of her skull and blood plastered against the wall behind her. The second RAID officer took a couple of steps forward and smashed the base of his rifle into the back of the kneeling man's shoulders to ensure that he couldn't move towards his fallen wife and detonate the bomb.

Leaving two men to watch the man, assumed to be the husband of the woman now lying dead in the main bedroom, the squad continued through the rest of the apartment. The contents of the rest of the flat were much as one would expect to find in a nice building in the eighteenth arrondissement. That was, except for the various components stored in one of the bedrooms, which the team immediately recognised as items that could be used for making deadly bombs to be left on the busy Metro.

Monterey – Tuesday, Late Evening

The American cryptic clue had led their teams to what appeared to be a very smart and expensive motor yacht tied up in the marina in Monterey. Monterey is home to a world famous aquarium, hosts its own annual music jamboree and is a great place to go and spot whales at certain times of the year. A small town with numerous bars and decent restaurants, it is a renowned tourist stopping-off point for those doing the drive up from LA to San Fran. It was hardly what the FBI expected as the place to go and look for those responsible for blowing up the Golden Gate Bridge.

Steve Brewer had insisted that Luke Ellis, the top man on the West Coast for the FBI, go down and supervise the operation personally. He didn't want any screw ups. There had been the normal politics involved about jurisdiction and whose team was better than the others, but on balance, given the location of the suspect boat, there had been general consensus that the local SWAT teams should be employed under Luke Ellis's control, in conjunction with additional FBI agent support. This ticked all the boxes; everyone would have a role to play in wrapping up this piece of the puzzle.

The target vessel was moored up at the end of one of the pontoons, its size meaning that it effectively took three berths to itself. This was good news as this kept it away from many of the boats tied up in the vicinity. The local police had cleared out a wide perimeter around the entrance to the marina, stating there had been a fight in one of the local bars so as not arouse too much attention. In practice this little ruse didn't hold for long as the arrival of a couple of SWAT vans and a helicopter suggested to the locals there was rather more than a pub brawl underway.

Two SWAT teams had been deployed from the shore side, whilst another team had been split between two Coast Guard vessels to ensure that no one could sail the boat out of the small harbour.

"Director, we're ready to go." Luke was standing near the end of the pontoon where the suspect yacht was berthed. He'd been working for the FBI for over twenty years and knew his business. Having made this announcement to his boss back in Washington, he once again reviewed in his mind the agreed plan and ensured that all the teams were in place.

"Good luck, we have all the live feeds in place," confirmed Steve Brewer who was watching the whole event unfold from the main operations room in the basement of the FBI headquarters. The room was packed with FBI operatives; TV screens would relay live pictures from various angles of the progress made in Monterey.

"We are go," instructed the onsite commander to the team leaders through their headsets.

It had been decided that it was impractical for the teams to approach unobserved. The option of putting men in the water had been discounted on the basis it would take them too long to climb up onto the raised pontoon or up the side of the motor yacht itself. The two land-based squads, therefore, made their way down the pontoon trying to find as much cover as possible as they went. They had signalled that they had reached the point of no return, by which time the Coast Guard vessel *Horizon* had closed to within seventy five yards of the yacht. *Horizon* turned on its powerful spotlights and trained them, along with a fifty calibre machine gun mounted on the front of the cutter, directly on the $2m yacht.

"This is the Coast Guard, anyone onboard the motor yacht *Inspire* should immediately come out onto the main deck with their hands raised above their heads. We warn you that we are prepared to use deadly force if our instructions are not complied with at once." The ship's speakers used would not have looked out of place at a Guns N' Roses concert and the volume employed ensured that anyone but the profoundly deaf would have clearly heard the instructions.

Nothing happened. The luxury yacht was showing a few lights below deck but otherwise there was no indication that anyone might be aboard. The instructions from *Horizon* were repeated in Spanish and in Arabic – again, nothing.

The two onshore SWAT teams cautiously continued making their approach; they had got within fifty yards when, without warning, the *Inspire* disappeared in a ball of flame. The shock waves buffeted the two Coast Guard vessels and managed to shatter a couple of windows; those on the pontoon were knocked backwards but otherwise escaped any serious injury.

"What the fuck!" Luke Ellis's voice could be heard across the SWAT team headsets and in the packed operations room in Washington.

The noise of the explosion reverberated up and down the marina. *Hell of a bar brawl*, thought a couple of the slightly inebriated members of the crowd that had assembled just outside the police perimeter line. Once the flames and smoke caused by the initial blast had receded, there was literally nothing left to be seen of the once pristine rich man's toy. The pontoon where the boat *Inspire* had been moored had also simply vanished.

It became very clear in a matter of moments after the huge explosion that there wouldn't be anybody to question about the San Francisco Bridge bombing; anyone involved that had been on the boat was clearly no longer available for comment.

Wandsworth, London – 02.00

Max had driven his supercharged Range Rover Sport hard across from Chiswick, making good time through the empty south London streets. On the way, Greg and Francois had checked their weapons; anticipating close quarter work they had opted for their SIG Sauer pistols and loaded up a couple of belts with stun grenades. The south circular was deserted at that time of night and apart from setting off a few speed cameras, *another thing for the Admiral to sort out*, mused Max, it was an uneventful journey.

Max parked the car in Hope Street a couple of hundred yards from the entrance to Usk Road.

They walked back towards where they believed the London bombing suspects were supposed to be living or at least staying.

"Greg you go down the far side, Francois come with me," instructed Max.

"Sure thing," said Greg. Crossing the road and sticking to the shadows as far as possible, he made his way slowly down the street. Five minutes later the team rendezvoused at the end of the road and compared notes.

From the quick reconnoitre, Max and his two guys had narrowed down the possible flats referred to in the cryptic clue to two alternatives.

"That's a bore," remarked Max. "I rather hoped that it wouldn't be a multi choice issue."

"How do you want to play it?" asked Francois.

"Not sure yet, in any event we're going to have to wait for a few minutes before we can go in," replied Max.

On the drive over, Admiral Walker had been insistent that they wait for some further backup and Max had reluctantly agreed.

Max started walking back up the road. "Let's go back to the car for the time being, I don't want to be seen hanging around here. The locals will think we're burglars and are casing a property."

"What, and call the police? Now that would be ironic," quipped Greg.

The three men walked briskly back to Hope Street. The Admiral had made the calls as promised and they didn't have to wait long for an armed unit of the Met police to arrive. The new arrivals had also parked their vehicles in the adjacent street so as not to alert the sleeping occupants of Usk Road.

Max shook hands with the recently arrived senior police officer. "Hi Lance, long time no see. How's life?"

"Yeah, good thanks, Max. I was very sorry to hear about Clare," replied the police firearms specialist. The two men had known each other for several years and whilst not close personal friends, as they mixed in different social networks, they had a great deal of professional respect for one another.

Max nodded his appreciation. "Thanks, she was a good woman."

Greg joined the pair. "What's the plan Max?"

"Ideally, we need to try and get someone out of there alive. We need some more information if we are ever going to find this 'Control' woman, if she even exists. I doubt somehow that the ringleaders are here." It hadn't sat well with Max that out of the blue they had suddenly been given a clue. It confirmed his suspicion that the news of Gary Stern's arrest had made it to the attention of whoever was pulling the strings. "The whole thing with messages being sent to us, the Americans and French in parallel strikes me as though someone is tidying up loose ends. I wouldn't be surprised if the bombers have been tipped off too."

"Makes sense," agreed Lance. He'd been with the Metropolitan Police for about ten years, since having left the army, and was a highly experienced and proficient officer. "From what I've heard from Paris, it sounds like the terrorists knew the game was up and that they were expecting visitors."

"That would tie in with what Patrick told us on the way over here. Apparently the suspect boat in Monterey was blown to smithereens before they could find anyone to talk to," added Greg.

Max took stock and thought for a moment. "Lance, how long would it take us to get a fire engine or two down here?"

"Not long," came the reply. "What do you have in mind?"

"Well, how about this as an idea? We dress up as firemen and wake up half the street on the basis there's been a gas leak and everyone has to get out of their houses."

"Go on," suggested Lance.

"Here's what I'm thinking. If we go in there with guns blazing we could end up killing civilians as well as any terrorists that we might find. Secondly, and assuming these are the real deal and serious terrorists, we might find a bunch of boys and girls who don't fancy being taken alive so we end up in a shoot out and or they find some way of blowing themselves, and all of us, to kingdom come."

"Fair point," commented Francois. He had spoken to Gerard in Paris a little earlier. "As Lance said, one of the people in Paris had rigged themselves as a human bomb, so I'm all for an alternative approach to getting shot or blown up."

Max started filling in some of the gaps in his plan. "If we get them out of the flat quietly, we'll see if they're carrying weapons and then we can get hold of them pretty easily. If they don't come out, then at least we will have evacuated the rest of the street. Thoughts?"

"How do we handle the fact we have two possible addresses to worry about?" asked Greg.

"We'll stick a couple of us outside each building. If they come out armed, we take them down hard, if not then we arrest them," replied Max.

"And what if they choose not to come out?" This time it was Francois looking for some more clarity on the action plan.

"We close off the building, check if anybody is actually in residence and sit them out." Max didn't have a better alternative for the moment.

Lance thought through the various options and possible outcomes , and seeing no obvious drawback in the logic, he said, "Why not? As good as anything I can think of, and I like the idea of drawing them out without them thinking the police are knocking on the door."

"Good, that's agreed then. Would you be good enough to make a couple of calls?" Max went on to add, "I need to let the Admiral and the rest of the team know what we're planning on doing."

"I'll get on with it." Lance got his mobile out of his jacket pocket and started to make the arrangements.

As promised, Max returned to his car and put a call into the office to update Patrick and the rest of the team on their plan. Fortunately, from what he could gather, everyone seemed basically OK with the approach.

Marylebone – Wednesday, 02.00

Petra and Alex had left an hour ago leaving Jo physically sated. She was wandering naked around her tasteful apartment, wondering what was going to happen today. This was the big day when all her careful planning would be put to the test, and the moment that her father would finally reap the just desserts of having been such a lousy parent and rotten husband.

She showered for the second time that evening and climbed into the guest room bedroom with its untainted, clean, cool, top quality satin sheets. She let her mind drift off to remember the time that she had spent in the Somalian terrorist camp where she had first conceived of her grand scheme.

When she had left Oxford with her first in History, she had decided to go travelling. Despite the occasional trip during school holidays out to far flung and, for the most part, exotic locations to spend some frigid time with her father, she had come to the conclusion that she knew very little about the real world. Her father would make little effort to make her feel welcome whilst he was on one of his interim assignments, and what should have been happy family time was anything but. Spending her time between private full-time boarding schools and unfulfilled true family life in the breaks left Jo bitter and desperately unhappy.

She was no fool and recognised early in life that her spoilt upbringing had sheltered her from the harsh realities of life experienced by the majority of the world's population. At the first opportunity, she took the chance to go and see the world for herself and on her own terms.

Almost immediately after graduating, and much to the annoyance of Lord Lockton, she had pointedly refused to accept his offer of a first class round the world ticket and had opted to hop on a lorry full of backpackers at Dover that was headed for Tibet. The experience had been an amazing awakening for her on every level; she had made friends and lovers on her trip. The eight month voyage of discovery had started by crossing Europe, down through the Balkans, across Turkey and then on through Lebanon, Israel, Syria, Iraq, Iran, Afghanistan, Pakistan, India, Nepal and finally arriving in Tibet.

There had been several hairy moments when their group had thought they were going to be robbed or worse by local bandits. They had no real means of defending themselves; in practice their unwashed look and apparent poverty made them low-grade targets for any modern day highway robbers. The many run-ins with various less than helpful border police was something to tell friends about on their return home.

The food had been awful, the sleeping condition primitive and trying to stay moderately clean almost impossible. There was a steady churn in the population in the truck as along the way some of the original members of the group had decided either to stay a little longer in one place than the schedule allowed, or simply had enough and decided to go home for a long hot bath. The number of young explorers in the old converted lorry stayed broadly the same, though, as new additions would be picked up as they continued their travels east. It was exciting and nothing like she had ever experienced. The crossing of the Bosphorus and onto another continent was something that she would never forget. She had loved every moment and the experience would shape her thoughts for the rest of her life.

What became ever more apparent to her was that one really didn't understand or appreciate sitting in London how the British were viewed from afar. The further she left London behind her, the bigger the differences would become between her perception of the UK and that of the indigenous populations. It was disconcerting how the modern history that she had learned and read about in such detail was many times at odds with the recollections of the people in the lands that she crossed. She started to open her mind to the distinct possibility that she had been brainwashed and misled at home. She began to reason that the local people in the countries that she had travelled through simply did not have a loud enough voice to be heard, and thereby could not ensure that their side of the story was told in full.

She was not so naive as to believe that everything that she had read or seen at home on the TV was the full story. During the months of travelling, she became ever more immersed in the local cultures and spent time talking with the elders of the villages where they camped overnight. It changed her in so many ways. She became committed to taking on the role of emissary for those people less fortunate than ones that she had grown up with, and would do all that she could to tell their story from their perspective. On the flight back home she had made her mind up that a career in journalism beckoned. She reasoned that would give her the platform to tell the stories that mattered and to do so in such a way that told the truth.

She had come back to London and unashamedly used her father's address book to get herself a job in News 24. In truth she was easily bright and talented enough to have got a job anyway, but she was in a hurry and so saw the use of his contacts as a quick way of circumnavigating the normally elongated process of finding a way into the media. Her bosses quickly recognised her obvious talent and intellectual bandwidth but were frankly taken aback when she insisted on working in the dangerous and gritty world of terrorism. She was fascinated by the old statement of "one man's terrorist being another man's freedom fighter" and she set herself the almost impossible task of reporting and writing about which of the alternatives, on a case by case basis, were true.

The experiences gained from reporting in 'trouble spots' around the world left her in little doubt that many of the western governments, particularly the Americans and their special relationship partners, the British, were still applying heavy handed imperialistic theology to solving the problems which frankly had little to do with them. The Americans and British, ably supported in many cases by the French, were the self-appointed policemen of the world. To her mind, it came as little surprise that many of the people affected by the strategies devised thousands of miles away from the reality of the current situations didn't like the unwelcome and uninvited involvements.

She realised early on in her career that overtly questioning the world police's stratagems was a quick way to lose her position in the media, and rationalised that she could spread the word more effectively by not being outside of the fold. The two months that she had spent in Somalia had been the tipping point. Frustrated that she was making little difference trying to provide what she considered to be balanced reporting, she reached the conclusion that the people sitting in their comfortable homes just weren't listening and she decided that she had to do something more attention-grabbing. Of course, her scheme would also have the added bonus of bringing down and destroying, once and for all, the house of Lockton.

Jo had developed enough of a reputation amongst the various terrorist organisations that she had met such that she was perceived not so much as a supporter, but someone who would at least make the effort to be a conduit for the messages that they were trying to get the wider world to hear. To most sane people tucked away in western society, had they known her true views and not the toned down TV friendly opines that she gave, she would have been described as having been brainwashed by the people that she had interviewed.

Somalia gave her the opportunity to devise her own grand scheme. Jo had gone into the desert to do a piece on the training camps that had been set up to educate prospective terrorists in the use of explosives and various other devices that could be used to inflict fearful damage on the imperialist West. She had met a broad range of people from all sorts of walks of life who, for any number of reasons, bore grudges against their various governments. Some of the motives for wishing to reap destruction were frankly laughable, others were more reasoned, and some budding terrorists were clearly simply there for the thrill factor.

Over time, she had independently befriended five or six of the weaker minded 'freedom fighters' as they liked to portray themselves. She decided that she would use them to deliver a cataclysmic message to the most obvious targets: America, France and the UK. Her message to the targeted populations would be simple and clear: 'Where there is a will there is a way and you will never be safe from home grown terrorism.'

A consummate story teller, with the financial resources and contacts in all the right places to get hold of the requisite materials to execute, she had carefully spun her web of deceit.

The west coast bombing had been set up with a couple of frustrated nationalised Americans of Arab origin. Their great mission was to attack an iconic landmark that starred on any number of postcards and that featured in holiday brochures around the world. She persuaded them that, by taking out the Golden Gate, they would be making a huge statement about how the indestructible was anything but and provide encouragement for their fellow 'terrorist' friends across the globe. Hiring a big truck had been a piece of cake, and how to make fertiliser bombs she found to be one of the most favourited videos on You Tube.

The men were naive in the extreme, came from a wealthy background and she found it almost inexplicable how easy it been to seed the idea in their heads. Of the four bombings, she had had reservations that they would actually go through with it. But they had and the pictures going around the world of the void where the Golden Gate once stood sent a message that everyone clearly understood.

The Paris Metro bombing had been carried out by a disaffected French family with connections in North Africa who were sick of being treated badly by the French Government. They wanted to lash out and demonstrate that problems further afield could be easily brought to the everyday Parisian way of life. Jo had been in London in 2005 when the tube and bus bombings had been carried out, and knew firsthand the trauma of bombing public transport would cause.

The planning had been straightforward and getting the explosives to the family had been achieved with the help of a German arms dealers and a couple of honest camper van tourists who had no idea what they were transporting across Europe. The mother had simply bordered a train at rush hour carrying a bag full of explosives, rode the Metro for a couple of stops, set the timer and got off. When they had received the tip off from Control that their cover had been compromised, the wife had decided to end all their lives before they could be captured by the authorities. She had killed their son and was preparing to blow herself and her husband up just as the police had entered the apartment.

Gary Stern was a complete psycho as far as Jo could determine; he had no real justification for wanting to become a terrorist as far she could establish, and he was the easiest of all the bombers to manipulate. In return for a few sexual favours she had persuaded him that blowing an aircraft full of innocent commuters would be the thrill rush of all time. He truly was a sick individual, a rabid dog and clearly should have been locked up by the authorities a long time ago. Getting hold of a SAM from one of her contacts had been a piece of cake; her biggest concern had been to make sure the clown didn't go and let the rocket off before the appointed date and time.

She turned to look at the bedside clock; the dimly lit numbers read 02.45. She was wired and finding it hard to sleep. Would people see her as psychotic terrorist or a messenger? Frankly she didn't care that much; she had seen so much death and depravation on her travels that the odd few hundred people killed along the way to change and potentially enlightenment seemed to hardly matter. Any number of times she had beamed satellite reports back to the studios in London telling of terrible stories of where complete innocents had been killed by misdirected bombs, or slaughtered as they slept by some crazed despot. What had become very clear was that the West put far more import on the death of a single westerner than an Afghan village disappearing in puff of high explosive dropped from 20,000 feet, a starving African, or some Palestinians being run over by an Israeli tank.

As she lay there, she recalled that the London bombers were two university dropouts who could have been on a gap year. *Perhaps they were,* mused Jo, *and they had just got on the wrong bus and ended up in Somalia by accident.* Products of decent middle class upbringings, Jeremiah and Gabriella for all intents and purposes didn't have a care in the world but raged at anything and everything. They were clearly deeply confused and vulnerable immature young adults who had struggled to build anything approaching a career at home. They were most likely a big disappointment to their respective sets of parents who had, by the sound of it, almost driven themselves to the verge of bankruptcy to provide their respective offspring with the private education that they never had. Why they had let themselves become convinced to get a complete stranger to take a large nail bomb onto a packed commuter train was a mystery? It was an unexpected result of their upbringing, as much to Jo as indeed it would be to those that knew them when the truth came out.

Four different insular groups; she had ensured that none of them knew that she was talking to the other 'teams'. All had one thing in common; they all demonstrated that they would show little or no obvious remorse for what they had committed to do and had indeed now done. Did any of them have a shred of legitimacy for the atrocity they had committed? Absolutely not, and that ultimately was, in at least Jo's warped mind, part of the lesson that had to be taught. Everyone and anyone could be made to become a terrorist, one just had to know which strings to pull in their psyche.

All life, irrespective of beliefs held or the colour of the skin was precious in her book. Did her actions make her the hypocrite of all time? She had considered the question many times, but ultimately had always concluded that one couldn't make an omelette without breaking a few eggs. The dramatic loss of life that she had instigated was an unfortunate necessity to make a point. The lives of those left behind would be changed forever, but in time their personal losses would doubtless be forgotten by the masses.

The message of vulnerability would live on and this aligned with the clear instruction to stay out of other people's lives that don't involve you would be etched into everyone's consciousness; at least that was her fervent belief.

Wandsworth – Wednesday, 03.00

The temperature had dropped further during the last hour and the assembled men were walking around flapping their arms to try and stay warm.

"Max, we can rule out the second flat." Lance was standing next to the fire engine which Max about to climb into.

"How so?" enquired Max

"We've checked it out, it belongs to a couple called Mr and Mrs Church," came the reply.

"OK, but how does that rule them out, Lance? We have to be sure." Max wasn't trying to be awkward but they couldn't afford to take any chances and let a suspect slip through their fingers.

Lance took a deep breath. "I appreciate that Max, he's in a coma and she's in the morgue so they're hardly likely to be suspects."

"You're kidding, they were on the train?" Max was dumbfounded.

"Yep."

"Unbelievable. What do we know about the occupants of the other property?" Max was still coming to terms with Lance's bombshell piece of news.

"Not much, short term let. To whom, we can't be sure," answered Lance.

"OK, let's do it!" Max climbed into the cab of the big red fire engine; despite himself he couldn't help being a little bit excited about driving a fire engine with all its bells ringing and lights flashing. He gunned the engine and switched on every bit of lighting he could find.

Looking all over the cabin he muttered, "Where's the siren for god's sake?" Greg had a quick nose around and pushed the button, and the siren began its wailing sound.

"There you go boss, happy?" said Greg with his trademark cheeky smile.

"Yep, thanks mate. Now hang on." Max ground the gears and pulled out of Hope Street.

The convoy of three fire engines roared down York Road and turned left into Usk Road. There were four men in every vehicle, and half a dozen men dotted in the shadows up and down the road.

Their arrival, as was intended, didn't go unnoticed; lights came on in the various properties up and down the normally quiet dead end street.

Jeremiah woke with a start. "What the fuck's all the noise about?" Gabriella, lying next to him, made the pointless gesture of pulling the duvet that they shared over her head in the vain hope of cancelling out the deafening noise from the street outside their window. The pair had been out drinking heavily the night before and then come back to their dingy flat south of the river to smoke some dodgy cannabis that Jeremiah had secured from a dealer in the local pub.

The man who had sent Jana to her death and, along with Gabriella's willing participation, killed several hundred innocent commuters, rolled out of bed and went to the window to see what was going on. "Looks like there's a fire or something, the road is full of fire engines." He turned and was making his way back to bed when they heard an insistent banging on their door downstairs. "Fire brigade, gas leak. Please evacuate the property immediately." The clear message was being repeated to the flat below them.

Returning to the window, Jeremiah could see several firemen in their fluorescent jackets walking up and down the street banging on all the doors. "Fuck, c'mon babe, get some clothes on we don't want to be blown up." Neither paused to remark on the irony of the comment; they were more concerned with saving themselves. Switching on the main bedroom light they both dressed quickly in the clothes they had been wearing the night before. With self-preservation at the fore they made their way down the stairs from their first floor flat and opened the front door. There were people milling around all over the place; from what they could tell, they were all being corralled back towards the river.

Max was standing at the end of the path that led to their door as the two suspects came out into the cold night air. "What's going on, mate?" asked Jeremiah as he approached the big fireman. "Gas leak, sir, any more of you in the flat?"

"Nah, just the two of us," Jeremiah answered pointing at Gabriella.

"Good." That was all the confirmation that Max required. He let Jeremiah and his girlfriend walk out of the gate and start following the rest of the residents of Usk Road. He and Greg fell in step behind them and pulled out their handguns. Satisfied that no one else was close enough to become embroiled in the scene, they prodded the snouts of their weapons hard into the backs of the unsuspecting London bombers.

"On the floor now! Stretch your arms and legs out," commanded Max.

"Hey, what's going on?"shrieked Gabriella.

"Get down on the floor, now!" Greg helped to ensure that she understood the instruction by giving her a sharp shove which pushed her to the ground. Both suspects on the ground and covered by the two men, two plain clothes police officers grabbed their wrists and cuffed them roughly behind their back. The two failed sociology students were bundled into a police van and driven away at speed to the high security police station just by Victoria Station.

Max and Greg quickly made their way back down the now deserted road and entered the flat marked as 1E. Taking the steps two at a time, with weapons still drawn to be on the safe side, they reached the landing area with four doors leading off. Max went forward and started looking around what appeared to be the bedroom. The whole place stunk of dirty linen, cheap perfume, cannabis and stale food. He had just about completed a fruitless search of the room when he heard Greg calling from another part of the grotty apartment.

"Max, come and look what I found."

Max walked back down the hall to the far end and in to what he guessed must be the kitchen. It was hard to tell because of its general state of disrepair but the cooker and fridge did at least offer a sensible clue as to its original purpose in life. "What have you got?"

Greg was standing near what could have been described as a food larder, not that Max would have recommended eating anything out of it.

"Look," said Greg, shining a torch into the back quadrant of the walk in food storage space come broom cupboard.

Max pulled out his mobile phone and dialled Patrick's direct line at the office in Chiswick. His call was answered on the second ring; Patrick and the rest of the now very tired team had been waiting for him to make contact.

Seeing the number pop up on the digital display of the conference phone, Patrick answered the phone comfortable in the knowledge of who would be on the other end. "Hi Max, this is Patrick. You're on the speaker phone. How did you get on?"

"The ruse with the fire engines worked well, we got everyone out of the properties including our two suspects from the apartment." Max paused for a moment. "Actually, let me rephrase that. What I meant to say was that we got the two sick bastards who were responsible for the bombing on Monday, without a shot being fired."

"Are you sure we've got the right people, Max?" Admiral Walker wasn't going to start celebrating any time soon before he had all the confirmations that he required to be sure they had the right people in custody.

Max, with Greg in tow, was now making his way back to his parked car as he replied, "Yes, Admiral. We found a stash of bomb making equipment in the kitchen along with a couple of ropey old pistols. Not sure what they were planning to do with the firearms, frankly the pair seem to be a couple of latter day hippies."

"OK, good work guys. We're going to call it a night here and try and get a couple of hours' sleep. Plan is to reconvene in Downing Street at eight thirty am. Does that work?"

Max checked his watch. 04.23. A couple of hours' rest was long overdue and most welcome. "Sounds good. Before I forget, there was also a mobile phone in the pack with an unanswered text message."

"What did it say?" asked Patrick.

"We've been compromised. C." replied Max.

"Interesting. Lucky for us they hadn't picked up the message or they might have been better prepared," commented Patrick.

"Possibly, but I'm convinced these guys are amateurs and they will crack easily once we start asking them some tough questions. See you guys in the morning." Closing the call, Max turned to Greg and Francois to update them on the meeting plan for the morning. Both men took up their boss's offer to crash at his place for the rest of the now very short night. Satisfied with their day's work, the men climbed into the supercharged Range Rover and put their seatbelts on for short drive to the barge moored on the Thames that Max called home.

Washington – Tuesday, 23.00

Steve Brewer, head man in the FBI, was in a foul mood. The Monterey operation had literally blown up in his face. He had no one to question regarding the San Francisco bombing and no leads for his men to chase down. The recovery operation in the bay was progressing, albeit slowly. In truth, he wasn't convinced that there would be much information forthcoming from the wreckage that they were pulling out. Making a fertiliser bomb was comparatively easily; building or buying the requisite explosive material to act as a detonator for the main bomb could be accomplished by a trip to almost any heavy duty hardware store. One man to drive the truck, another possibly on the boat. *Who knows?* he thought. For all he knew the boat in Monterey had been rigged to blow anyway, and it would be several hours before he would get any definitive answer on whether there was someone on board the *Inspire*. "Fuck, what a mess," he said out loud.

He picked up his phone and dialled the number of Field Agent Bourne in Boston.

"Gina, has that fucker Stern woken up yet?" The Director of the FBI was keen to try and wring some more information out of Gary before he was completely wrapped up and protected from further interrogation by his new favourite lawyer friend.

"No sir. They brought him out of surgery a couple of hours ago and the doctors tell me he should regain consciousness in the next thirty minutes of so," was FBI Agent Bourne's reply. She wished that she had more to add.

"The Brits have sent over a pack of possible suspects and they want you to show them to him and see if he'll help us, and himself, by pointing out who the bitch is behind these outrages." Sitting at his desk in the FBI's head office, Steve Brewer flicked idly through the 180 sheets that had been sent through from London. "I've forwarded the documents to you so you can print them off or show them to him on the screen as you wish."

"Yeah, I've got them, thanks," Gina confirmed. She took another turn in the naval hospital corridor and made her way back to where the armed guard was sitting outside the terrorist's room. On her way, she passed the lawyer that had been sent out by Harris and Harris to defend the man. He was keeping himself busy flicking through the report that Gina as the arresting officer had put together, and the medical report. He looked up as she passed and gave her a small nod to acknowledge her presence.

"Sir, I'm going to have a chat with his lawyer and see if we can at least get him to take a look at the photos under no obligation," suggested Gina. She was pretty convinced that unless it was done in such a way that there would be no admission of guilt on Gary's part, he simply wouldn't offer to help.

"Good idea, let me know how you get on." Steve punched the button on his speaker phone and the line went dead.

Gina returned to where the lawyer was sitting. "Andrew, can we talk?"

He looked up from the paperwork on his lap. "That would depend on what it was about. Reading through this material," he tapped the pile of paperwork, "my client has got a rock solid case to sue the assoff this Max Thatcher, whoever he is, and the FBI, for not doing anything to prevent him being beaten up and knifed."

Gina recognised that she was most likely going to have an uphill battle trying to get this man to work with her. "Look, Andrew, I know you have a job to do." She almost choked on the words but it was clear that taking an aggressive line was going to serve little purpose. "You can't seriously expect me to believe that you have, in truth, any sympathy with the man lying in the room down the corridor."

"He's entitled to his civil rights, Agent Bourne, and they have been clearly violated," came the unhelpful response.

Doing her best to remain calm she pressed on. "I'm not saying you're right or that you are wrong in that regard, Andrew. All that, at least in my opinion, can be for another day. Right now, I've got a man who has confessed to blowing up a passenger jet bound for New York killing some two hundred innocent people. The fact that the law chooses to protect him from having the truth extracted is a moot point for now." She waited for a response.

"Go on, I'm listening." As a highly paid defence lawyer, Andrew Chalmers had had to defend a number of clients for whom he had little or no regard. The man lying next door was clearly a complete fruit case, and he acknowledged that it could easily have been him sitting on that fateful flight heading for a meeting in New York.

"I am going to need your help to find out if he recognises any of the photos of some people that we believe could be the main orchestrators of the bombings here and in Europe." Gina believed she saw a spark of hope that this man might be prepared to work with her.

"What do you have in mind, Agent Bourne?" asked the defence lawyer.

"Please, call me Gina." There was more than a glimmer

"OK, Gina. What do you have in mind?" At least it appeared that she had his attention.

"We show him the photos on the basis that we ask him to point out the person or persons that he recognises. We don't ask him why he knows them ... OK?" Gina knew that this 'unofficial' identity parade wouldn't stand up in court but frankly, she didn't care. If they knew who to go find, they could always work out the rest later.

"What does my client get for helping?" Andrew was always looking for a deal; it was his job.

Gina almost despaired, she felt like saying something along the lines that perhaps the doctors who had just saved his client's life might not be so considerate going forward and let the fucker die. Instead she thought for a moment. "How about we agree not to go for the needle?"

"Well, that assumes the man is guilty, but I suppose we could agree that in the event that this came to trial that the death penalty was not an option." It seemed like a decent deal to the Boston based lawyer. "I'll talk to him when he comes around and see what he says, fair enough?"

Gina wasn't overly enamoured with the principle of doing deals with a terrorist who had confessed only a few short hours ago, but she was at a loss what else to try. Getting Max back to carry on another interrogation in his own personal style probably wasn't an option.

"OK," she said begrudgingly. She walked down the corridor to make a couple of calls to make sure that her superiors were prepared to back her up. Bottom line was, even if they weren't going to be, she'd lie; to hell with her career. She wanted the person behind the atrocities more than she wanted a pension.

South London – Wednesday, 06.00

Alex was wearing a smart pair of beige chinos and a heavily checked shirt; he'd showered since his physical exploits with his two female playthings earlier that morning. He was all for equality amongst men, but where women were concerned they were there to bear children and look after their men folk. That was how his father had raised him, and he saw no reason to change.

He looked around the poorly lit warehouse set in between the railway lines just to the north of Clapham Junction His neighbours, a mixture of lockups and rather dubious car body shops, kept to themselves. People came and went all day and sometimes late into the night so it was easy to come and go and he didn't attract any unwanted attention when, as he had now, he assembled his group of handpicked freedom fighters.

Over the years, since his parents had been indiscriminately murdered by the unseen American bomb, he had dedicated himself to bringing terror and death to various western countries. The focus of his efforts had invariably always been around the French, Americans and British; those that he held most responsible for the loss of his family. He had been a young boy when he had been left all alone on the side of the mountain and had to fend for himself. It wasn't long before he had been recruited by a terrorist group and completely indoctrinated to hate the West. He had been taught to kill, something he found easy to do and indeed relished; he felt no remorse for taking life.

By the time he was in his late teens he was a complete fanatic; he didn't hold any particularly strong views on religion but rather considered himself to be his own messenger. Eventually, even the leaders of group that had taken him in became concerned with their ability to control this young man, who seemed intent only on killing on the least pretext. Frustrated that he was only playing on a small stage in his native lands, he decided to travel and become an independent, working with anyone who could help provide financial or material resources to allow him to continue his one-man vendetta. He was a 'gun for hire' to anyone who shared his intense dislike for his preferred targets, and he offered his talents happily.

The group of men in the warehouse were the dregs of society in most sane people's books; they were mercenary thugs who got a thrill out of what they did in the name of whatever cause was prepared to endorse their terrible actions. The majority were frankly there only for the money.

Alex had recruited the majority of the group over the last six or seven weeks. It hadn't been hard, the most important element of the recruitment process was not to inadvertently pick up one of the myriad of undercover agents that the various secret services around the globe tried to seed into the terrorist networks. He had found, over the years, that he was better off using people who did not fall into the zealot bracket; they tended to be to idealistic and one ended up in a negotiation. He had no interest in debating the validity of one cause over another. In truth, all he wanted were people that would follow orders without question.

The rag tag bunch of misfits that stood in front of him on that cold January morning were from a very broad spread of different countries and with mixed religious backgrounds. He didn't care; understanding a man's motivations was key in learning how to control that individual, and finding people who were greedy for personal wealth was the simplest leverage point in his experience. He had gone into the 'market' looking for guns for hire who would be lured into the plot by the promise of a large cut of cash for a successful conclusion to the project. Robbing banks was all rather passé these days, and the opportunity to steal heaps of cash was severely limited by all the new tricks and devices that the banks used to mark their cash. Stealing in today's economy was more a 'white collar' crime, less violent and more intellectual. This left a pool of resources who had little to do other than hire themselves out as mercenaries, and even in that market segment pay rates were going down.

The secret services tended to focus more on the better known terrorist cells where they would set out to insert their operatives as 'volunteers'. Indeed one of his favourite roles had been acting as a 'cleanser'; he would be engaged to vet new recruits and indeed sometimes long standing members of this or that organisation. He had a knack of seeing through people and was adroit at hunting out moles and spies. Doubtless some of the people that he put against the wall and blew their brains out had indeed been genuine supporters of the faction that they had committed their lives to. The reality, of course, was once they were dead no one could ever check, and so his reputation preceded him for complete ruthlessness and efficiency. He was a resource in demand, never stayed with any group for any length of time and drifted along just below the radar of the security services.

For the London operation he had picked out other loners; some he had met on his travels and others were recommended to him by the odd person that he trusted. Only one had aroused his suspicions, an Italian guy who had seemed just a little bit too switched on and inquisitive about the ulterior motives. Once someone started digging around his business or pushing for information past how much money was on offer, he would become suspicious. He replayed in his mind how he had met Paulo in Rome at the end last year; initially he had seemed to be a really good candidate.

Alex had walked into the square at the appointed hour and made his way to the cafe where the meeting had been arranged to be held. The afternoon sun was still shining on the eternal city. Walking up to the table he extended his hand.

"Paulo?" He recognised the man from a photo sent. Unusual; Alex absolutely abhorred any picture being taken of him.

"Ciao, Blake?" Alex never used his real name with his employees. Paulo rose from the chair that he had been sitting on in the Piazza Navonna and shook Alex's hand. The weather in September had still been very warm and both men were dressed in short sleeve shirts and chinos.

"Good to meet you, Paulo." Alex took a chair with his back to the small cafe that they were sitting outside. He would prefer to have his back hard up against a wall, but on this occasion he had little choice. An attendant waiter came over and asked what he would like to drink. "Espresso, grazie." Alex spoke any number of languages; it helped him drift unnoticed from country to country.

"Subito." The waiter disappeared into the dark of the cafe.

Alex took a look around him; the Piazza was fairly busy as usual. A mixture of local artists selling their wares to gullible tourists; what started at 150 euros could easily be bought for less than 30 euros if one had the patience. Most of the artwork on display was churned out by the local student community who used it as a way of paying for their food and drink.

"So tell me, Paulo, how did you come to find my name?" Alex had received a cryptic note suggesting the meeting via an acquaintance a few days earlier when he had been in Germany; he had few, if any, people that he would call friends.

"I was speaking to a friend and heard that you are looking to put a team together for some work in the near future." Paulo adjusted his sunglasses so that he could take a closer look at a scantily clad young woman who walked past where they were sitting. Alex was interested in the man's language syntax; it didn't sound natural Italian but rather more English American. So not a native Italian, at a guess, or educated overseas to a very high degree, which was rather inconsistent with a mercenary.

"That's half an answer, but not the answer to my original question." Alex's coffee arrived. "Grazie."

"Prego." They were left on their own again.

"I don't like to pass names around if it can be helped," said Paulo with a little smile.

A cautious and discrete man; Alex liked that, switching into Italian. "I fully understand, but unless you tell me we are going to have a very short conversation."

"Ummm, OK, but you understand that it would be embarrassing for me if it were to become public that I shared a contact." The Italian was perfect, but no accent. This man wasn't a born and raised Italian. Alex's warning sensors kicked off in his head. "His name is Rudi, a German that I have worked with in the past."

"I see, would that be Rudi Geller? I haven't seen him for years, still living in Cologne?" The surname and city were both made up by Alex.

"Oh, he is very well. I met him in a bar in Koeln and shared a beer or two with him." Paulo delivered another lie with total conviction.

Appearing to buy the lines, Alex threw one more qualification into the mix. "He loves the local beer. Oh, what's it called? Weiss something or another if I remember correctly." Alex had visited Koeln many times, and he was pretty fond of the famous local Koelsch. Weissbier was more of a southern German drink.

"Yes, you must have a fantastic memory," beamed Paulo. He clearly hadn't ever been near Koeln, and who the hell Rudi Geller was was a complete mystery to Alex. Three strikes, this man was a plant of some description.

Alex made a point of checking his watch. "Look I have another meeting in ten minutes over near the Spanish Steps. I'm staying at Cavalieri up on the hill, perhaps we could meet for a drink and some dinner there at, say, eight pm?"

If Paulo was disappointed to have the preliminary meeting cut short, he didn't show it. "Sure, that sounds great." *Definitely American*, decided Alex.

Alex rose and made to leave a few euros for his coffee. "Please, let me take care of that," offered Paulo.

"Grazie." Alex made his way out of the square and headed towards the Trevi Fountain, which in turn would lead him through the narrow streets towards the Spanish Steps. He made no effort to check whether he was being followed; it was at least, in his mind, a near certainty.

Alex enjoyed Rome; literally everywhere you looked there was history to be seen. Since the end of the Roman Empire, the Italians hadn't spent a lot of time off conquering far flung parts of the globe. They had their odd outposts primarily in Africa, notably with interests in east Africa in Somalia and Ethopia, but for the most part they concentrated on their fine wines, great food and beautiful women and of course their cars.

Upon reaching the Spanish Steps, one of the world famous tourist attractions for which Rome is suitable famed, Alex made a point of hanging around as though he were waiting for someone. Ten minutes of apparently fruitless waiting had passed when Alex got the opportunity that he had been waiting for. A large coach load of what appeared to be American tourists passed by and Alex took a couple of steps into their midst. He then cut down Via dei Condotti, a fairly narrow street which was full of bustling tourists and locals. Thirty yards along, he cut into a narrow passageway and waited. Sure enough, within ninety seconds Paulo came wandering by; he was making little pretence of looking innocent and appeared agitated, presumably because he had lost the man he was supposed to have been following.

Satisfied that Paulo, or whatever his real name might be, was on his own, Alex slipped out of his hiding spot and followed in the man's slipstream. He slipped a garrotting wire out of his belt and held it curled up in the palm of one of his powerful hands.

The shadows had lengthened by the time Paulo had made his way down to the river; not knowing in which direction Alex had gone, he'd clearly decided to simply take a straight line back towards the fabulous five star hotel where Alex had said he was staying. In Alex's experience, both the police and security services rarely considered top class hotels as a likely resting place for terrorists.

Paulo crossed the Tiber at Ponte Cavour and made his way in the general direction of the Vatican City. It was pretty clear that he was just aimlessly wandering around now and had given any hope of relocating the elusive Alex. The crowds had disappeared on this side of the Tiber and the light had all but deserted the day. Paulo was about to give up and was meandering through Piazza Cavour, a predominantly pedestrian area, though at this time of day it was empty apart from the palm trees that looked so attractive in the tourist shots.

"Hello Paulo." Alex had come up quickly, unnoticed behind the man and slipped the wire around the man's neck. He pulled it tight, lifting Paulo briefly off his feet and pulling him backwards into the dark shadows of the local fauna. Paulo desperately tried to claw at the wire, which sliced easily through his skin and bit deeply into his neck. Alex was a powerful man and highly proficient with a garrote; he liked the fact you had to get up and close with the intended victim. He enjoyed the futility of the struggles as the thin cheese wire severed the wind pipe and then the main blood-carrying arteries in turn. Paulo's eyes dimmed as his life blood ebbed away. Alex checked through the man's pockets and found a US passport in the name of Attino, first name John. He took the passport and emptied the wallet of cash.

Alex killed with no remorse; John Attino was another victim of his ruthless nature. He would check with his contacts whether the man was, as he believed CIA. It was of little consequence, as Paulo had in any event clearly been lying about how he had found Alex. Alex would have let that go and simply disappeared, but that the man had been foolish enough to follow him had resulted in the suspected agent effectively signing his own death warrant. The fact that someone known to Alex had passed on his name to such a man was something of a concern, and he had resolved to find out who that was and deal with the matter appropriately.

Alex returned his thoughts to the day's operation; fortunately the rest of his recruitment process had not been so bloody.

There was no heating in the warehouse and the exhaled air from the assembled group created a small cloud above their heads whilst they stood and listened attentively to Alex's final briefing.

"We will enter the building as planned; secure the doors and round up the occupants in the newsroom. Kill anyone that does not comply immediately." He was standing on an upturned crate so that the fifteen heavily armed men would have an uninterrupted view of their leader.

"Blake?" said a man called Grant who had been at a loose end since being thrown out of the army for drug dealing in Afghanistan. "The part I'm not clear about is how we get out of the building. We get in no problem, but once we're there the police will surround us and we'll be trapped."

"We've been over this any number of times, Grant. They will not dare come into the building whilst we are holding all the hostages, and once the ransom has been paid we will exit the building through the sewer systems under the building."

"I get that, but how on earth do we get into the sewer to start with?" Grant for one found it hard to understand how the group could make into the pipe work that was laced beneath the streets of London.

Alex stepped down from the crate and made his way to the table where a floor plan of the building had been spread out. "Look, on the plans there is a large expanse under the building where all the communications and computer servers are stored." The group crowded around. Alex then brought out a map of the sewer network. "Here's the building." he pointed to the diagram. "We will blow a hole in the floor of the basement and drop down into the sewer. We will disappear and be gone long before they've worked out what we've done."

There was a general nodding of heads around the group; it really hadn't occurred to many that an exit strategy was rather a key part of escaping with the ransom and not spending the rest of their lives behind bars. The majority of the group were basically totally reliant on the fact that Alex must also want to get out, so he must have had a plan. Grant wasn't finished. "Blake, that's all well and good, but what happens if we can't get through the concrete?"

The leader snapped Grant a sharp look. "That's what those rucksacks over there are for." He pointed at a pile of bags stacked in the corner of the warehouse. "I have explained this before, were you not paying attention or you questioning me?" Alex's reputation for total ruthlessness and short temper preceded him. The disgraced former soldier thought better of continuing the line of enquiry. "No, Blake, I've got it. Thanks."

Alex spoke to the whole group whilst still holding the now very frightened man's eye. "Good, we go in," he checked his watch, "just over six hours. Make sure you bring all the explosives, Grant perhaps you could take care of that?" It wasn't a request.

"Sure thing, Blake," responded Grant, delighted with the opportunity to be seen as playing an intrinsic part of the operation. Hopefully Blake, as Grant knew Alex, would forgive him his indiscretion of asking too many questions.

Alex moved away from the group and went into the small room that would originally have been used by the warehouse manager as an office. Closing the door behind him and satisfying himself that he couldn't be seen by any of his ramshackle troops, he doubled up in pain and collapsed, exhausted, in a chair. The attacks were, as the doctors had predicted, getting worse. One moment he would be absolutely fine the next he would have excruciating pain in his head and could barely speak. The brain tumour was inoperable; he had no intention of escaping or even trying. This was to be his last mission, his last act of wanton violence and destruction; all to be carried out live on television and broadcast to the millions of viewers around the world.

He took out a small phial of tablets and tipped four onto his hand. The dosage should have been two a day but he had little concern for what the doctors said; the pain was debilitating and he only had to get through a few more hours.

Whitehall – Wednesday, 08.30

The team from the night before had reassembled. There were a couple of additions to the group, most notably the Prime Minister, who was chairing the meeting. Bacon sandwiches and cups of coffee or tea had been brought in to help replenish the 'troops'. This was particularly good news for Greg and Francois as it was pretty clear that Max's bachelor pad contained little in the way of food. For that matter, all three of them were starving, and they did a pretty good job of finishing all the supplies in short order.

Rupert Taylor looked like he had aged ten years in the last forty eight hours; he had expected stress to come as part of the job but nothing like what he had experienced these past couple of days. His suit and shirt may have looked as though they were neatly pressed and had recently returned from the dry cleaner but his face was drawn and the bloodshot eyes evidenced his lack of sleep. He was either in the 'House' (Houses of Parliament) explaining to the members of parliament why no one had been caught yet, or he was doing the rounds of TV studios. He knew it was very important to convey confidence to the general population and, for the most part, political commentators thought he was doing a pretty good job. Any 'spare' time was taken up on calls with his counterparts across the globe, in meetings such as the one he was now chairing, taking care of bodily functions or getting the occasional cat nap in before he collapsed completely. He was tired, fed up with the lack of progress and was beginning to wish that he had never got into politics in the first place.

He called the meeting to order. "Good morning ladies and gentleman, judging by the looks of you all we've all got some rest to catch up on with when we resolve this problem." There were a couple of tired nods in response. "Charlie and Jessica, please may I ask that you update and take us through where we are in our investigations?"

Jessica gave a quick quizzical look across the table at her opposite number; Charlie nodded his assent so as to indicate that he agreed that she ought to go first. This little exchange was not missed by Admiral Walker, who was pleased that the respective heads of MI5 and MI6 were obviously working well together; this hadn't always been the case. It had never ceased to amaze and indeed irritate the Admiral in equal measure that organisations which were ostensibly doing the same thing, namely looking after the security of the UK, would frequently not work together or communicate for the common good. The fact that one had a domestic slant to its operation whilst the other concentrated on international espionage shouldn't, at least in his mind, have prevented the organisations working closely together. Several times over the years he had had to step in and almost physically restrain the respective heads punching each other's lights out in arguments over whose jurisdiction a certain matter fell within. The Admiral used to go to great lengths to explain that everyone was, in fact, in the same boat and it didn't matter what end the hole was in; if it didn't get fixed everyone was going to be in dire straits.

At least Charlie and Jessica seem to be working well together, which was a bonus. He tuned back into what the head of MI6 was saying.

"Prime Minister, the French 'clue' led them to an apartment in the eighteenth arrondissement." A couple of people gave her a blank look. "Montmartre for those of you who can't remember all the post codes of Paris," she said with a smile. She then continued, "It would appear that they had been tipped off to expect company. According to reports, when the police arrived they found a young boy murdered and the boy's parents apparently arguing in another room. From all accounts it looks very much as thought the mother was about to blow herself up along with half the neighbourhood. Fortunately she didn't get the chance and was shot dead by the police before she could detonate the vest that she was wearing."

Admiral Walker shook his head and silently mused over how parents could kill their own son and then contemplate killing a whole bunch more innocents. He was a naval man and had seen his own fair share of live action over the years. As a young man, he'd had personal experience of seeing death up close and, as with most trained soldiers, took no pleasure in witnessing or indeed having a personal involvement in killing. For his part his career in the services had always been involved with other armed combatants, or at least people that had a pretty good idea of what they were doing and knew the risks. He just couldn't comprehend what was going through other people's minds, such as the French tube bombers, at times like these. In his book, killing innocent people with no warning was beyond reason.

"The police have the husband in custody and he has confessed to the bombings." Jessica paused to see if there were any questions. Most of this was not new news to the group, so in the absence of any requests for clarification she continued. "The French police have pressed him hard to tell them who was behind the bombings. Not much new news or progress in this regard. All they could get out of the husband was that the person who had helped put the whole plot together was female, spoke with an English accent and that they had met her last year at a training camp in Somalia."

"Have the French police showed him the photos that we sent over yet?" asked one of Charlie Marsh's MI5 contingent present in the room.

"Yes. Apparently he didn't recognise anyone from the album. It appears that most of the time 'Control', as he knew her, was wearing a full burkha. So all we've got is average height, weight etc and olive eyes ... not much use in truth," replied the head of MI6. In truth, the description given by the bomber had come as little surprise. She knew from long experience that even people who lived with another person for a long period of time would, in many cases, simply come up with 'average this or average that' as a description.

"Disappointing. What else have you got, Jessica?" asked the Prime Minister. He wasn't looking forward to another session with the press and not having anything concrete to report. He secretly considered that maybe on this occasion he'd send one of his junior ministers to go and bask in the limelight.

"Charlie will cover off the UK suspects. As far as the USA is concerned, the Californian connection is a dead end. The suspects again were tipped off and before they could be captured opted to blow themselves to kingdom come." She gave a brief overview of the FBI mission in Monterey before moving on to the situation on the East Coast.

"The Boston terrorist is under heavy sedation," she took a quick look in Max's direction, "not expecting to hear much from that quarter until later in the day, if then." Jessica took a look around the room and shrugged her shoulders as if to say 'sorry' but there wasn't much more that she could add to the picture.

"Thanks for that. Charlie, what have you got from the pair that Max picked up last night?" Rupert longed for something to work with.

"They haven't said that much yet, we've got them locked up in the high security police station at Victoria." all the assembled knew that this was where terrorists or highly dangerous suspects were held for questioning. "We've established that they don't have any sensible explanations for where they were on Monday morning. We're checking through the CCTV for Clapham Junction to see whether either of them turns up there. I realise that we are looking for some new news but would ask for a little more patience. We have a bit of time, as you can imagine we're holding them under anti-terrorist legislation so we won't have to charge them for a couple of days. I would also agree with Max's assessment last night, they'll not take long to crack."

"Presumably we are still searching further afield than simply looking at the CCTV for Clapham Junction? They could just have easily boarded anywhere else on the train's journey in?" asked Max.

"You make a very valid point Max, but as it's the nearest point to where you found them we decided that we had to start somewhere and it's such a time consuming process that we can't do everything in parallel. Hopefully we'll catch a break."

"Charlie, what else turned up at the flat?" asked Greg.

Charlie was as frustrated as everybody else and his tone showed it. "We've been over the flat with a fine-tooth comb, apart from the stash you discovered we found some drugs and that was about it. Regrettably, nothing connecting them to a particular individual."

Max chose to recap for his own benefit as much as anyone else's. "So we've got Boston, Paris and London bombers under lock and key. Nothing to go on as far as San Francisco is concerned. We know that they are all connected by a woman called 'Control' but we don't know who or where she is apart from she has an English accent. 'Control' is possibly a reporter of some description and has at some point visited a Somali terrorist camp which is presumably where she recruited the bombers. That about it?"

"I'd say so," replied Admiral Walker, the silence from the other members of the meeting confirmed that Max's summation was on the money as far as they were all concerned.

"Still not an awful lot to work with," mused Max

Jessica had been reading an email from her counterpart in the US. "Chaps, one more new piece of information to add. The FBI have found an instruction booklet for a shoulder-launched SAM in Gary Stern's apartment."

"You must be kidding, just how stupid is this guy?" It never ceased to amaze Max how daft people could be. Why on earth would you keep an instruction booklet for a SAM missile? *Maybe as a souvenir,* he thought. The police were going to have a field day with that little gem.

Charlie echoed his thoughts. "Well the good news is that ought to add a bit of leverage to their questioning. I can't see that there's much justifiable cause for keeping a SAM in your bedroom or on your boat in that part of the world!"

"Agreed. So where do we go from here?" queried Max.

Rupert Taylor was the first to offer an opinion. "I guess from my perspective I want to make sure that we're not about to have another round of bombings. We obviously need to work out the 'how' and try and get some more details on the 'why' but public confidence is fragile to say the least, and another train bombing would be terrible on several fronts."

"I agree," said Admiral Walker. "There are more people back at work today but from the reports I've seen some fifteen to twenty per cent of the workforce are still staying at home. Clearly this can't go on; it'll help when we publicly announce that we have suspects under arrest. However, I share the PM's concern that without getting hold of the orchestrator behind these atrocities we could easily end up with another bombing today, tomorrow or whenever."

Max had been looking through a ring binder containing the profiles of possible candidates to be the as-yet highly elusive Control. "How many people are in here?" he asked, pointing at the folder.

"183," answered Charlie, the head of MI5.

Seemed like a big number to him. "How on earth do we narrow it down from here?" asked Max.

Charlie responded, "We're going through each suspect and determining whether there is sufficient material or information about them to warrant further investigation. Right now we've got a team doing a lot of desktop research and individual profiling. It's a long, laborious, time consuming process."

Rupert's heart sank further; going through detailed background checks on 183 individuals would take an inordinate amount of time. He wanted and indeed needed quick results, but at the same time fully recognised that without being thorough in the process it would be a pointless exercise.

"Fair enough, any idea when we'll be finished with a first pass?" Max was keen to get a look at a shortened list and then maybe go help interview some of the suspects.

Charlie considered for a moment or two. "Realistically we might be through the list within 48 hours, tops 72 I would estimate. We'd then take the shortened list and refine it further ..."

"Hang on," interjected Patrick, "the file we started looking through last night contained 209 suspects. What's happened to twenty six names?"

"I don't know," admitted Charlie, the question had caught him a little off guard. "I imagine some of them have been discounted already."

Patrick was not going to let this pass that easily. "What new information have we received since last night that would have ruled out twenty six people? I've not seen anything, have I missed something?" His tone indicated that he wasn't at all happy about the apparent lack of agreed process.

"Steady Patrick, maybe some of them are dead or just not that likely." Greg sought to mollify his friend's tone.

"What's your point, Patrick?" asked Max.

"Max, it's pretty simple really." *This'll be a first*, thought Max to himself privately. Patrick had a great ability to think laterally and often left his colleagues behind when he made some of his simple – in Patrick's mind - jumps in logic. On this occasion, though, it seemed to be more of a domestic housekeeping, and therefore mundane, issue that had got Patrick excited. "Look, at least in my opinion we had very few parameters to work with when we came up with the initial search criteria. They weren't narrow enough to come up with a handful of people but neither were they so broad that we had a list of a couple of thousand." Patrick paused.

"Not sure I follow your point, Patrick," said Rupert. "Surely not having a great long list to start with is a good thing?"

Patrick refrained, only just, from rolling his eyes. "PM, with respect, the point is that we don't have a huge sample to start with and even then our pool of suspects is, at least in my opinion, quite possibly too small and we simply can't therefore rule people out without due cause. I also thought that we had agreed that NO name was to be removed without full discussion by this team. So I repeat, what new information has materialised?"

There was silence around the room as though it were a classroom full on naughty school children that had just been told off by the Headmaster for breaking school rules.

Everyone looked around at the head of MI5, the most likely candidate for having got the rest of the class in trouble. "Charlie?" asked Admiral Walker.

"None that I'm aware of. I'll find out what's happened for the list to have been changed," responded Charlie.

"Thank you," said the Admiral. Continuing, he asked, "Patrick, you've been through the original list. Are there any profiles which stand out in your opinion?"

"I have had a cursory look through. A few caught my eye." He referred to his notes. "Chadwick, Frazer, Feigen, Hummerich, Lockton, Parsons, Stevens, Wilkins and Young."

The Prime Minister picked up the folder that Max had been studying and scanned the list at the front which had the entire contents listed. "There's no Feigen, Lockton or Young in here."

"Full names, Jill Feigen, Josephine Lockton and Janice Young," quoted Patrick from his document set.

Rupert couldn't believe his ears. "Jo Lockton, the TV reporter? She's on the list? You must be kidding? Her father is Lord Lockton, I've been shooting with the man. No wonder her name was taken off the list. Waste of time tracking someone like that." He was beginning to wonder who this Patrick fellow was.

"With respect, Prime Minister, just because you see her on the TV and she's the daughter of someone you go shooting with is no reason to take her off a list," Patrick answered in a level tone.

The PM rolled his eyes. "Whatever, but complete waste of time in my opinion."

"Noted, Prime Minister, but nonetheless I would like her name re-included please." Patrick was polite but adamant.

Max saw immediately where Patrick's train of thought was going and decided to jump in and perhaps open the Prime Minister's, and indeed the rest of the room's, eyes to Patrick's potentially brilliant piece of insightful thinking. "Stockholm Syndrome, Prime Minister, ring any bells?"

"Vaguely, but what has Lord Lockton got to do with any of this?" The PM disliked, in common with most people, being questioned in public about his point of view.

Max continued. "If I may, let me refresh our memories. Patty Hearst, heir to a family fortune, was kidnapped by terrorists in the 1970s. In return for her release, her kidnappers demanded that the family pay over millions of dollars to feed the less fortunate in California. Can't remember all the precise details but apparently some monies were paid over eventually. Actually I believe it was agreed by the family that rather than money they would help the poor directly. Long story cut short Ms Hearst was not released and was then quoted as saying her father could have done better on the quality of food distributed. To cap it all, a couple of months later she turns up robbing banks alongside the very same people who had kidnapped her. Point being that it is entirely possible for the least likely people to become mixed up with, or in the case of Ms. Hearst, be turned by, terrorists."

Begrudgingly the Prime Minister concurred, but wasn't going to resist having the last word. "Patty Hearst was American and not the daughter of a Lord of the Realm. OK, put her back on the list." Almost as an aside, he added under his breath, "I'll owe her father a huge apology when he finds out."

This last comment piqued Patrick's curiosity. "Excuse me, Prime Minister, but how's he ever going to find out?"

The PM was putting his files together and getting ready to head off to another 'crisis' meeting this one with the PR people. "Oh, simple really. Lord Lockton sits on one of the security sub committees. He gets copies of all COBRA meetings," replied the PM.

"Oh Christ," said Max.

Colin Street, South Bank, London - Tuesday, 12.45

Alex had insisted that his band of mercenaries make their way by taxi to the meeting points in small groups of two of three men. The police had stepped up security at all the major railway stations and there were random searches taking place on the underground. His group would undoubtedly have attracted attention if they were all seen together. The attack was scheduled for just under two hours' time; all was in place.

Whether the explosives his men were carrying would be sufficient to blow a hole in the floor to connect them with the main sewer was of little consequence to Alex. He knew that there was easily enough explosive material to bring the whole building down on top of everyone, a fitting epitaph for his career.

He checked in with the various team leaders dotted around the area and, satisfied that all was as it should be, made his way down the street and towards the TV studios.

In his opinion London was a comparatively easy target to bomb; everyone was so nice and trusting. When he had carried out bombings in other parts of the world he had had to take far more precautions. In less stable countries it was an accepted norm that one could be stopped and searched on a whim. In a large cosmopolitan city like London it was straightforward to merge into the background, people left you alone and didn't choose to enquire what you were about. Never having been directly associated or affiliated with any particular terrorist group, Alex had always managed to stay off the various security radars. He could travel as he wished and was able to move around in public with little fear of being stopped by the police.

It had come as a devastating shock when the doctors had told him that his life would be ending in the next nine months. He wondered whether the brain tumour was some form of divine retribution for all his terrible actions. Ultimately his almost atheistic lack of belief in any greater being had convinced him that it was simply bad luck and he had decided that he would end his illustrious career on a high.

Persuading Jo had been laughably easy; she knew nothing of his medical condition and simply wanted to believe that her 'freedom fighter' shared her belief that delivering a short sharp shock to the chosen governments would change how they behaved on the world stage. Alex was under no such illusions; his messages in his damaged mind were not deemed to be of an educational nature, but were ones of bloody revenge and no more.

He would go to any lengths to inflict as much death and misery on the people that had took his family away from him. He cared little for the various causes that he had, over the years, purported to support with his lethal actions. He was only sorry that natural causes were going to cut his life short and with that the ability to carry on killing and maiming.

He checked his watch. Less than an hour to go.

News 24 TV Studios, South Bank London – 14.00

The main lunchtime news bulletin had been delivered as usual at its appointed one pmslot. Dominated, as it had been for the past three days, by the various bombings around the world, the news channel had decided to spice things up a little and put together a 'Terrorism Special'. The audience engrossed watching the weather forecast for the UK, which had just been completed, was a record figure. Apparently, it was going to rain for the next week and the current spate of flood warnings in place from the Environment Agency was due to increase from the current tally of sixty odd to over a hundred in the forthcoming days.

Following the obligatory commercial break, the live video stream returned to the news studio and focused on Control sitting next to a coffee table with a distinguished looking man in his early seventies. A seating area had been arranged in front of the curved news desks and one of the three available chairs was left open, presumably for the next guest.

Jo looked radiant. Through the glass topped table she could see on a TV monitor her live, perfectly manicured image being beamed in to households and offices across the world. News 24 had a huge following not only in the UK but across the globe. The ultimate parent company was a massive American corporation which used its not inconsiderable financial and marketing muscle to ensure that the channel was well subscribed to in every major territory worldwide.

Normally at this time of day, the live feed would be split into US-centric news and European-focused events but because of the 'international' bombings earlier in the week, the channel had decided to put on the 'Terrorism Special'. The hour long programme would be shown live across all their distribution channels simultaneously. It had been something of no brainer who should play the lead role; who better to host the show than their worldwide terrorist expert, Jo Lockton? She was, needless to say, ecstatic; this was much better than she could have hoped for.

The program kicked off with a small 'sting' - "A News 24 special report, brought live from the London offices of News 24," boomed the voice over. Tens of millions of people around the world settled a little more comfortably in their chairs, or wherever they were perched, to watch this much publicised programme.

"Good afternoon, my name is Jo Lockton and I will be your host for the next hour as we go in to detail about the bombings earlier this week. First: a recap of what has happened in London, Paris, Boston and San Francisco. I must warn you that many of the images will be disturbing to some of our viewers." Her head and shoulder shot was replaced as a video tape was run for the next four minutes detailing the atrocities committed by as yet unknown people. She had argued vociferously with editorial team on the content of the video. The final edit, to her bitter disappointment, had in the end been something of a compromise, with some of the more gruesome shots of wanton death and destruction left on the proverbial floor of the editing suite.

In any event, she was pretty sure that the four minute tape had done its job and grabbed the viewing public's undivided attention. The camera focused on her perfect complexion. "Hard stuff to watch, but, ladies and gentleman, very real-world." The director in the control room looked at the teleprompter material that Jo was supposed to be using; she must have ad-libbed. The material was a bit dark for this time of day, he thought, but the producers and Jo had wanted this slot as it gave the programme the opportunity of fitting in across as many time zones as possible.

"After the short break I will be asking Lord Lockton, Chairman of the Commonwealth oversight committee on security," the director switched to camera two so that the guest could be seen sitting next to the show's presenter, "to help us understand better how such dreadful events have been allowed to happen and what can be done to stop these types of events." Camera one was brought back in to play as Jo gave her best smile directly into the lens for the close up shot. "And yes, before you all write in, he is my father!"

The director in the control room was puzzled; she was broadly on script but had digressed a couple of times from the agreed text.

After being urged to buy cars, look for cheaper car insurance or possibly go on a lovely holiday to get away from all these nasty bombs and foul weather, Jo's twenty million or so UK viewers - a record for this type of programme - were ready to be informed. As Jo had anticipated, the UK viewing figures were swelled by the large number of people who had decided not to run the gauntlet of commuting to work. Worldwide she had managed to amass a global audience approaching one hundred million, all of which were now focused back, after receiving their own sponsored 'local messages', into what she and her guest were about to say.

Lord Lockton, dressed in one of finest handmade Savile Row suits, fidgeted nervously in his chair. He didn't like or trust the media. In his view, they had a habit of only telling one side of the story. Indeed, his well-publicised after family dinner opinion of messages not being delivered properly had been, at least in part, his downfall. Jo had innocently given him the opportunity to come and tell his side of the story on national or rather global, TV; what could be fairer? So a mixture of his own big mouth and not a little bit of wishing to be in the limelight had led him to the 'hot seat' to be interviewed by his own daughter. A tight script had been agreed and as far as he was concerned, there were no surprises in store.

"Lord Lockton." It had been agreed that she could hardly call him dad or father. "How do you think the bombers managed to place their devices so easily, despite all the tax payers' money being spent on national security?"

There she goes again, thought the program director, *off script*. She was supposed to have started with a question about what the authorities knew about the current death toll.

Lord Lockton decided he would stick to his appointed lines. "Josephine, to begin with, I would like to express our deepest sympathies with all those families that have lost loved ones or are still in hospital receiving treatment for the terrible injuries they sustained at the hands of these wicked people. We are also very cognisant of the terrible loss of life in France and the United States, and we wish to unequivocally extend our heartfelt condolences to all those caught up in these terrible events." He thought that went rather well.

"Noted," though those watching doubted she had done any such thing, "and doubtless your words will bring great comfort to the people affected." Everyone in the studio noticed that there was more than a touch of sarcasm in Jo's voice. The sharp look from her father, picked up by camera two, indicated her tone hadn't been lost on him either. *This is going to be fun*, thought the show's director. He gave up watching what was going round on the teleprompter; she was clearly on her own agenda.

Lord Lockton was an old pro and was not going to allow himself be riled that easily by his daughter. He continued in a level tone, "As I was about to go on to say." *Touché*, thought the occupants in the control room. "The government obviously takes very seriously the security of its citizens both here and, I would like to stress, also when they abroad." He took a sip of water from the glass on the table; he clearly wasn't going to be rushed.

Looking directly at his daughter as if to add weight to his comment, he said, "You," a slight pause, "and all your viewers doubtless appreciate that we have to find a balance between providing a suitable level of security and not becoming a police state. It's impractical, and frankly not desirable, to implement such stringent security measures that it becomes impossible for people to go about their normal lives."

Jo was having none of it. "Would it be fair to say that on this occasion that the police and secret services failed? A train load of people have been blown up and we, the tax paying public, have no idea about the who? Or the why? Which suggests that the government doesn't know anything either."

Was this really the best she could come up with? Lord Lockton was visibly relaxing and appeared completely comfortable batting away these highly simplistic questions and observations. He was, however, somewhat stung a little by the suggestion that those in power were not in the know and decided to show off a little.

"Actually Josephine, we have a pretty good idea about who the terrorists are and in conjunction with our colleagues in France and the US, we have undertaken a series of coordinated actions that have resulted in a number of suspects now being under arrest."

Control gave no indication that she already knew. She had planned this interview vary carefully along the lines of a game of chess. She was keen to lure her father into a false sense of security and would let him take a couple of her pawns. She knew full well that his vanity and pride would cloud his judgement, and that the opportunity to demonstrate to all how much clever he was than the lowly TV reporter, albeit his daughter, would be irresistible.

"That's good news, who are the suspects under arrest in the UK?" asked Control sweetly.

Bugger, thought Lord Lockton. He rather regretted having let on about the arrests. Indeed, in the briefing he'd gone through before coming on, he had been told in no uncertain terms not to divulge anything regarding the arrests. He tried to extricate himself from his self-created hole. "Our enquiries are still underway so I'd rather not say any more about it."

"C'mon, Lord Lockton, are we talking about one, two, ten? How many people have been arrested in the UK?" She had him very much on the back foot.

Another sip of water, this time to try and generate a bit more thinking time. "I really wouldn't want to say, it's a matter of national security."

"Men, women, ethnic origin, where ...?" Jo was enjoying herself.

Lord Lockton decided to keep silent rather than dig a deeper hole for himself.

"OK, so as you have no response, we'll assume that it's a matter of national security that we are not entitled to know who blows up our fellow citizens." Jo enjoyed, almost more than anything, goading her father. The fact she that could do so on live TV to a record audience simply made the experience that much more pleasurable.

"I didn't say that ..." blustered her father; his face had turned puce in colour and looked like it might be about to explode. He might have been about to say something more but forgot the cardinal rule that the person with the metaphorical, though in this case physical, microphone invariably has the last word and the attention of the audience.

"You see, Lord Lockton. I, and I suspect many of the people watching this programme, have become a little confused over what is subject to national security and what isn't. It seems entirely reasonable that we have a say in how much security there is on the streets, and similarly when the police make arrests, we ought to know."

Lord Lockton was trying to regain a modicum of control in the proceedings, or at least stop his daughter from pushing him around quite so easily.

"Josephine." Jo had insisted prior to the interview that he call by her first name rather than Ms Lockton. It would, and did, create the desired impression that he was lecturing her in a patronising fashion. His tone did nothing to remove the impression of being very condescending. "Clearly there are some subject matters that cannot be discussed in the public domain. And we have to decide what gets shared and what is kept secret."

"Who's we?" asked Jo innocently. She was pretty sure that by now, the vast majority of her audience would think that she was getting very evasive answers from a patronising old fart.

"The government of the day in consultation with the heads of the various departments that help keep our country safe." *Where is she going now?* he wondered.

"And if we the public never get an insight in to this process, or a say of any type, how can WE be sure that the right calls are being made with regard to what should or should not be made public?" She had him boxed.

Lord Lockton had no ready answer for that one, she knew it and the rapt audience around the globe knew it too. Check mate!

After what seemed like an awkward silence lasting minutes, but was in truth only a few short seconds, Jo turned away from her father and looked into camera one.

"Don't go away, after the break we're going to meet a man who can tell us how a suicide bomb works." That was an offer that was bound to keep the audience glued through the commercial break.

Whitehall – Wednesday, 14.25

The latest 'crisis' meeting had been wrapped up about an hour earlier.

Charlie had been given clear instructions with regards to ensuring that a full profile on Jo Lockton was put together immediately. To Max's mind she could easily, along with a number of other people on the list, be a prime suspect. She quite possibly had had access to sensitive information via her father. In her role, she had visited any number of terrorist sites during her career and had she been turned, like Patty Hearst, on any one of these trips, could easily have become the mastermind behind the bombings.

Patrick and Max, with no immediate work to keep themselves occupied, had sat themselves in one of the myriad meeting rooms and decided to do a bit of their own research on the only child of Lord and Lady Lockton. The TV Special hosted by Jo Lockton had been well-publicised during the last twenty four hours not only on the news channel itself but also on the commercial radio stations and in the press so at two pm sharp they had switched on to watch the show.

Max had been watching Jo's performance intently looking for any tell-tale signs. Patrick had tuned in and out whilst scanning through the internet and any other sources of information he could lay his hands on.

"She doesn't like her father, does she?" observed Max.

"No, that's putting it mildly. I would think, from what I've seen and heard in her tone of voice, that she loathes him." Patrick continued, "She's had a first class education, first at Oxford, disappeared off the radar for a while and then reappeared as a news reporter. Very few women reporters in her field of specialism."

"Not surprised, bloody dangerous I would have thought, and many of the people she would wanted to have interviewed would have had little time for a woman at all," commented Max.

"I agree on both counts. Must be a pretty gutsy lady."

In the background, Jo's voice could be heard asking people not go away and to look forward to finding out about the intricacies of suicide bombing after the break.

"Hang on a minute!" The larger of the two men suddenly becoming very agitated.

"What is it, Max?" asked Patrick.

"Did you say that she had been to Kurdistan?"queried Max.

Patrick looked back at his laptop screen "Yes, Bukan," he pulled up a map off the internet. The sketched out region of Kurdistan, not a country in its own right, came up in a couple of seconds. The area had inherited its name from the fact that the majority of the inhabitants were Kurds. Both men stood looking at the screen. "A bit of a no man's land by the looks of it, Northern Iran and Northern Iraq borders just south of Armenia," said Patrick.

The commercial break was coming to an end on the TV mounted on the wall opposite them. "I know the area, Patrick, there's no way she'd have lasted more than ten minutes as a single woman without a sponsor. If she's heavily involved in these bombings, and I'm beginning to think she's potentially a good bet, then we're looking for two people, not one."

They both looked up from the computer screen.

"Welcome back. In the next half of the programme we're going to focus on suicide bombers ..."

Max tuned out of what Jo was saying; his mobile phone was vibrating insistently in his pocket. He didn't recognise the number but saw from the international code it had originated in the States. He slid the answer bar across on the iPhone. "Max Thatcher."

"Max, it's Gina Bourne."

The TV special continued. "I'd like to welcome Alex Berwari to the show ..." Max was watching the TV and listening to Jo and Gina in parallel.

"Hi, what's up?" enquired Max.

"We know who it is." Gina's last statement got Max's full attention.

"Who?" demanded Max.

"Gary Stern identified Jo Lockton!" said Gina triumphantly.

Max tapped Patrick on the shoulder and pointed at the TV screen. "I've got Gina Bourne on the phone, the guy in the states pointed out Jo Lockton from the deck we sent over." He headed out of the door with Patrick following close behind.

Gina had heard what Max had said to Patrick. "Actually Max, her photo wasn't in the deck." Max guessed that only the shortened list had been sent.

"How did he identify her then?" Max and Patrick sprinted through the Whitehall offices leaving startled people in their wake. They made their way out of the building and onto Parliament Street. Patrick hailed a taxi whilst Max continued his call with the FBI Agent. Gina quickly explained what had happened. "You won't believe this but the sick bastard wanted to watch the big exposé on News 24. He obviously got a sick thrill out of watching it being replayed and talked about on the TV."

"Why doesn't that surprise me? But the programme started half an hour ago, did he only just say something now?" Max was trying to figure out why it had taken so long to make the call.

"Sorry Max, I was out of the room for the first bit and then I had to call my boss. I only found out ten minutes before I called you." Max could hear the remorse in her voice, hopefully the ten minutes lost would not prove to be important later.

The taxi was crawling in heavy traffic across Westminster Bridge, Max pulled out his SIG Sauer P226 9mm pistol and tapped the window separating himself and Patrick from the cabbie. The driver turned to see what was going on. "Fuck me guv, what's all that about?"

"We're police, mate, and I need you to get us to the News 24 Studios at South Bank like fucking grease lightening. Got it?" Max's size, tone and gun seemed to do the trick as he was thrown back into the seat as the taxi accelerated forward with lights flashing and horn blaring.

"Good luck Max." He still had the mobile pressed to his ear. "Sounds like you're on your way somewhere in a hurry!"

"Thanks." He cut the call.

The next call he made was to Admiral Walker.

News 24 Studios, South Bank –14.38

The commercials finished and viewers around the world tuned back in to Jo's voice. A new man had joined the father and daughter on the studio set.

"Welcome back to this special report on global terrorism. My next guest is man who has experienced firsthand what drives people to become suicide bombers ..."

Jo had been looking forward to this part of the show; the finale was approaching. She had met Alex a long time ago on her first voyage of discovery, in the lorry that she had initially border in Dover.

Alex was five years her junior but had seemed to her so much older and wiser than his eighteen years when he had joined the touring group in Turkey. His life appeared far more exciting and full of purpose than her own had so far been. He had told her all about growing up in the mountains, the son of a poor Kurdish family. He was strong as an ox with big thick set shoulders and rough hands used to manual work; he told her of his dream to be free from the yoke of various countries who would never allow the Kurds to have their own sovereign nation. This was, had she but known, only one of the many stories he liked to roll out to fit his purposes.

It was in his arms after they made love, which they did frequently, that he had convinced her that the only way to make things happen was to take direct action, and that was why he had committed himself and his life to fighting those that oppressed his fellow men. As Jo had shared with him her unhappy upbringing, and the lack of love from her father in particular, he had preyed on her weakness. He had shown and gone to great lengths to convince her how important it was to become independent. By the time they had finished their stint of travelling together, she had become as much of zealot as he was. Over the years they had kept in touch and she had helped him and believed in his people in whatever way that he had asked. For the most part, this had normally involved sending money, but when she could she did very one-sided reports about the plight of the Kurdish people.

When he had come to London a little over a year ago and suggested it was time for her to take a more direct involvement, she had taken little persuasion to do something to scare the populations of the UK, France and the United States. It was important that she show them how vulnerable they were and that they were at risk because of the actions, or lack of action in some cases, that their governments took. She was in love with Alex and would happily sacrifice all for him; in her book he was a true freedom fighter.

"Alex, what do you believe makes a person sacrifice their lives by blowing themselves up?" asked Jo.

"Desperation, Jo, and in some the belief that the ultimate sacrifice will ensure that they go to their heaven." Alex smiled warmly at the presenter of the Special Report.

Lord Lockton sat on the far side of Alex, away from Jo, and was beginning to wonder why he hadn't insisted on leaving at the last commercial break. As far as he could ascertain, the man sitting between him and his daughter was not to be trusted. His answers were a little too well rehearsed and delivered too smoothly without any apparent pause for thought; it was almost as if Jo and Alex were going through a pre-prepared routine.

"One of the things that has always fascinated me, Alex, is what these devices actually looks like up close. I believe we have a little surprise in store for our audience," she said with a naughty school girl smile.

Lord Lockton looked towards the TV monitors dotted around the studio, expecting a picture of video to appear. The programme director was at a loss as to what was going to happen next.

Alex stood up and removed the heavy sweater that he had been wearing.

"What the fuck?" The director in the control room was left open mouthed.

All around his clean shaven barrel chest Jo's lover had what appeared to be slabs of explosives which were all wired together. The bomb had been smuggled in through the building's kitchen area; no one thought to look for a bomb in a sack of potatoes. Over the top of his macabre vest, he was wearing what looked like a waistcoat of ball bearings. Directly above his solar plexus the wires all came together joining in a small junction box which was topped with a button. It was flashing red.

"Are you crazy, is that a live bomb?" demanded Lord Lockton, now standing on his feet.

Jo remained seated during the whole disrobing process and beamed with pride at her man.

"Jo, what the fuck is going on?" screamed the director in the control room situated some forty feet from where the live bomb was standing.

Jo jumped to her feet. "Jerry, you touch one button or consider cutting the live feed and Alex will detonate the bomb, killing everyone in this area. This means you too! And before you think about getting cute, I can see the live feed on the monitor in front of me."

All her planning had come down to this, the big moment when she could reveal her true nature and deliver the message that so desperately needed to be heard.

Including sound technicians, camera men, floor manager and various lackeys there were some twenty people within the probable immediate blast area. Jerry sat transfixed; in any event, he wasn't sure that he could have made his legs carry him out of the room. The newsroom, on the other hand, which could be seen through the soundproofed glass behind where the presenters normally sat, was emptying rapidly.

They weren't going to get far. As planned, all the exits to the building had now been closed off by heavily armed members of the terrorist group. In total there were close to four hundred people trapped inside the building that housed the news studios.

Thanks to the power of the internet and mobile telephony, it took less than three minutes for the global viewing audience to expand rapidly from seventy to over one hundred and fifty million totally engaged people. This was free entertainment of the highest order; in fact, some of the people tuning in later had mistakenly taken what they were seeing on their TVs as a movie and not real life.

Max walked with Patrick at his side into the back of the control room; both had drawn their weapons.

"Fuck, we're too late," muttered Max.

"Looks that way," conceded Patrick.

"What happens now, Josephine?" Her father had decided to sit down again.

Alex provided him with a less than welcome answer. In a well-practised manner, he took off the waistcoat and explosive vest. "Stand," he commanded Lord Lockton.

"Now, look here," said the man as he got shakily to his legs.

Alex slapped the much older man hard across the face. "Stop whining." Despite herself, Jo couldn't help but flinch as she saw her father being struck.

The terrorist expertly re-positioned the bombs on the aging Lord. Satisfied with his work, he pulled a small radio out of his pocket and inserted an earpiece so that the other end of any conversation would remain private. Speaking a mixture of Arabic and English, he ensured that the various parts of his small private army were in place around the building. He instructed his men to corral all the people from the three floors of the building into the large newsroom behind the set that he was on.

Jo sat and watched Alex at work. She was relishing being in the middle of it all and looking forward to telling the world why she had done what she had. Hopefully, they would listen and there would be justice for Alex's people.

She stood and went to stand by the man of the moment, the freedom fighter she adored and that had she had given up everything for, including her father. He turned and looked down at her; she mouthed silently, "I love you." The sneer of pure contempt that was her reward for her heartfelt expression of true love hurt far more than the back-handed slap she received.

"Get away from me, you stupid western bitch!"

He father went for the man. "You bastard, you leave my daughter alone or I'll kill you!"

"Ha, you silly old man. She was prepared to see you die!" Alex easily avoided the old man's oncoming rush and pushed him to the floor. "Try that again and I'll cut her throat!!"

"Alex, what are you saying? This was all about helping your people." Jo's mind was in complete turmoil.

"You fool!" came the harsh response. "Now sit down and shut up!"

Back in the control room Max whispered to Patrick, "Looks like a lovers' tiff, mate."

Patrick couldn't resist a small snigger. "Yep, the path of true love is never easy. What do you figure we do?"

"For now we play it cool, tuck your gun away. There are bound to be more of his guys around. Let's see how things develop. We need to get at that bomb and defuse it before he blows up all these people."

"Agreed," said Patrick. Both men put their weapons back in their shoulder holsters, which were well concealed under their outdoor jackets.

Max walked up to Jerry. "This man," he pointed at Patrick, "and I are secret service. In the next couple of minutes I'm guessing some goons are going to arrive and empty this room. It's imperative that you convince them that Patrick and I are necessary to run the show. OK?"

"Got it," confirmed the rattled Jerry.

The newsroom behind the glass screen was filling up as Alex's men herded up the occupants of the building. As Max predicted, three terrorists came into the control room brandishing AK47s.

"Who is in charge here?" demanded one of the men.

"I am," said Jerry with a wavering voice.

"Everyone but him out!" shouted the man at the rest of the control room occupants.

"Hang on," said Jerry; he then pointed at Max and Patrick. "I need these two guys to keep the lights on or the programme will not continue to be shown."

"OK, the rest of you go!" The leader of this group left one man to guard the three men remaining in the control room and continued rounding up other News 24 employees.

Downing Street, London – Wednesday, 15.35

"Prime Minister, we're going to have to make a call on what to do about the feed." Charlie Marsh was sitting at the large oval - and recently much overused - meeting table in conference room A. The COBRA meeting had been convened in short order following the unbelievable turn of events on live TV that many had seen f first hand. "The Americans have held off switching them off but that won't last for much longer."

"What can they tell from within the studios? Will they know if their coverage is getting through?" asked Admiral Walker.

Jez Smith, one of News 24 producers fortunately not to have been in the building at the time, had been brought in to provide advice to the rest of the group, and provided the answer. "From the floor of the studio they can only see what's happening on a local circuit. For example, what's showing in the UK. In the newsroom," he pointed to the large 60-inch screen that had been brought into the meeting room, "that area behind the glass they have TV screens showing every major distribution channel. So long story short, yes. We start switching them off and they'll see it straight away."

"How about getting into the building?" asked the PM.

"Tricky, the building has seven entrances of various descriptions; four main doors, two fire exits and a delivery-come-loading area at the rear of the building. These now appear to have been secured by armed terrorists," replied the head of MI5.

"How many terrorists do you reckon are on the ground?" enquired the Admiral.

"Best guess between fifteen and twenty, details are sketchy sir," replied Charlie. "We have the place surrounded and as you know we believe that Max and Patrick may have made it inside, though we've had no contact with them since Max called you on the way over there."

"Prime Minister, you need to see this." Jessica drew the room's attention back to the large screen.

There had been comparatively little action for the last thirty minutes or so. Jo could be seen sitting next to her father who was wearing the suicide vest. Behind them the watching masses could see that the newsroom was full of people who had been made to sit on the floor. The prisoners were surrounded by eight or nine men, all of whom were wearing balaclavas and pointing their guns menacingly in their general direction. Alex had disappeared out of shot for the past fifteen minutes; he had gone to make sure that all the explosives were placed correctly in the data communications room beneath the main newsroom. He'd set the timer to detonate the bomb for ninety minute hence: 17.28 GMT. The free agent terrorist had now returned to the main stage and was standing behind Jo and Lord Lockton. The leader looked like he was to about to address his audience.

"Turn the volume up," instructed the Prime Minister.

"... taken over these studios on behalf of the FAUKSUR terrorist movement. We are proud of the bombings that we have orchestrated this week; these are only a taste of what we are capable of if our demands are not met. Don't be foolish enough to believe that we do not already have other plans in place. My family was killed at the hands of the Americans; their blood will be forever on the hands of the people who ordered bombs be dropped on innocent civilians. You will make amends or everyone in this building will die. Our demands ..."

"So these are the bastards behind this week. Who the hell are the FAUKSUR terrorist movement?" demanded the PM. He received only blank stares from around the room.

Alex's voice continued, "... are simple and must be met within the next four hours ..."

Here we go, thought Admiral Walker. "... firstly the imperialist America will release all freedom fighters on the list that we have sent to the American Embassy in London. Secondly, the British government will deliver to these studios $5bn worth of industrial diamonds, and finally, the French government will remove all its troops forthwith from the Central African Republic. These terms are not negotiable and must be complied with in full before," he checked his watch, "Eight pm London time."

The COBRA members sat in stunned silence; this turned to shock as Alex indicated for a young female News 24 employee to be brought forward and made to kneel in front of the cameras. "We have shown that we are capable of destruction and acts of terrorism on a global scale. Now witness firsthand what will happen to all of the people in this building if you cut the live picture feed or if our demands are not met."

Alex was handed a large machete. The young woman's scream of sheer panic - she knew what was coming - was cut short as the madman hacked her head off in three heavy blows.

The woman's headless torso was dragged away to a corner of the studio, leaving a trail of blood in its wake. Alex picked up the head dripping blood. "You have your instructions!" He threw it casually in the general direction of where the rest of the body had been dumped.

"That's one sick fuck," said Jessica to no one in particular.

News 24 Studios – Wednesday, Afternoon

Jo's head was in a complete spin, it had dawned on her all too late that Alex didn't love her, never had and that she had been played for all these years. *Oh my god, what have I done?* She had almost been physically sick when Alex had executed the young TV researcher in front of her. Jo had known the girl, Beth Childs, a nice kid just starting out in the industry who, because of her actions, was now lying decapitated in the corner of the studio. The very place that the poor girl would have dreamt about reading the news from one day. All those people dead around the world, and she had been an instrumental part in the whole scheme.

Jo got out of her seat and began to follow her lover, the man she considered her mentor for most of her adult life, out of the studio. "Alex, what are you doing? This was supposed to be about freedom and making people realise just how vulnerable they were." She knew that there was no chance of America or France complying with the demands made; they were totally impractical and were never going to happen. The demand for money in the form of diamonds was the only instruction that anyone could comply with, and even then she very much doubted that the UK government would kowtow in public to terrorist demands.

The original plan, or so she had thought, was for her, Alex and her unwilling father to make the ultimate sacrifice and blow themselves up on live TV to prove to the world just how far desperate people were prepared to go for the great cause. Freedom was the ultimate dream. Freedom for a small sovereign nation from the oppressive yoke of imperialistic actions of the three governments that they had picked to target with their wanton acts of terrorism. Jo believed that by showing, to 100 million people, the effects of their governments' actions, she could force foreign policies to be changed.

Alex turned and faced Jo. His look was one of hatred and contempt; she could hardly recognise the man that stood in front of her. "Everyone will die here, everyone that is watching with morbid fascination on the TV sets will never forget the name FAUKSUR – they will fear us all over the world. We will strike everywhere; they will suffer pain and death brought about by my brothers and sisters. We are in a war against every nation that involves itself in the lives of others outside of their own borders. We are the troops of the weak, the deliverers of retribution."

Jo stopped in her tracks. "You're insane."

"As you said yourself, Jo: one man's freedom fighter is another man's terrorist. We are the freedom fighters for the poor; the ones who can't afford to rise up. We will extort money from the rich, not to give to the poor but to fund our campaigns of terror against the imperialistic pigs. Now stay out of my sight, or you will be the next person I use to demonstrate our ruthlessness."

Video Conference Suite, Downing Street - Wednesday, 15.55

"Rupert, there is no way that we are going to agree to any of their ludicrous demands." the American President could be seen sitting in his private office in the White House. The Director of the FBI could be seen sitting on his right.

"We agree," the French President concurred; he was sitting at the end of a long table with his cabinet members framing him in the centre of the picture.

"I thought as much, and I can confirm that the British government is of a similar mind. Our analysis is that this group could quite easily be a suicide squad and that they have no intention of negotiating, but are simply using the platform to spread their anarchic views across the globe." Rupert Taylor, with the heads of both MI5 and MI6 for companions, leant back in his chair.

"What are you proposing to do, Prime Minister?" asked Steve Brewer

"We're going to switch the feed off in an hour's time and go in hard," replied the British PM.

"There's going to be terrible loss of life," stated his French counterpart.

"We see no alternative, regrettably." Rupert didn't like the prognosis. His analysts had predicted that they would be doing well to get any of the two hundred or so hostages out in one piece. The alternative of being held to ransom by terrorists was not an option.

"Good luck, Rupert." the American President was pleased that it wasn't his terrible responsibility to effectively condemn so many to death, but could see that his British counterpart had little choice. He would of course make the point, had this been happening on American soil, that he too would have taken such decisive action.

The screens went blank. The British Prime Minister sat back in his chair and held his head in his hands. Admiral Walker got up from his chair and put a comforting arm around the man who was effectively signing the death warrants of several hundred innocent people.

"Rupert, you have no choice. We don't negotiate with terrorists, whatever the potential loss of life is. Once you enter into a discussion with these animals we open the door for copycat attacks all over the place." The old soldier had been impressed with the PM's handling of the meeting held earlier when the decision to go in had been made. He knew it was a terrible decision to have to make and ultimately, whilst all the members of the group had supported the option, it would be the Prime Minister who would take responsibility and carry the burden with him until he died. The PM alone would have to be the one to console the families of those that had lost their lives and answer the question that would be repeated countless times. "There must have been an alternative?"

"Thank you Gordon, I know there's no choice but it doesn't make it any easier." The career politician was holding himself together, just.

A knock at the door interrupted any further private discussion. "Yes," snapped the Admiral.

Jessica walked into the room. "I'm sorry to disturb you both but may I have a moment?"

The Prime Minister pulled himself together; he was a very different man to the one that he had been only forty eight hours earlier. His demeanour now carried more weight and gravitas in public; he was learning his trade of being a leader of the country in the hardest way possible. As Admiral Walker had accurately judged at the beginning of the terrible business, these events and how they would be addressed would be the making or breaking of Rupert. In the Admiral's considered opinion, the man was going to get through and would be all the stronger for the experience.

"Sure, what's on your mind?" asked the PM.

Jessica slipped a disc into of the screens on the desk. "May I?"

"Go ahead," instructed the Admiral.

"We've been studying the video tape from the broadcast and there's something which doesn't make sense to the team." Patrick pushed the play button. An enlarged section of video could be seen on the screen. "If you look past Lord Lockton, you can see several hooded armed men carrying large bags." Both the Prime Minister and the Admiral nodded.

"And?" enquired Rupert.

"We think they are carrying explosives," said Jessica. "There are too many bags to be simple munitions and they're not going to have brought in packed lunches."

"You think they're planning on rigging the studio?" asked the PM.

"Well, that's what we thought initially, but look. All the bags have been taken out of the room and we can't be one hundred per cent sure but it looks like their hostages have not been wired up." Jessica paused.

The Admiral stood up and went to take a closer look at the screen. "What do you make of it, Jessica?"

"Here's what I think. If they were planning on hanging around for any length of time and dissuading us from attacking the building they would have made a big point of telling us that the hostages were all going to be blown up if we made a move. So far, the leader has made no such threat. The fact that he's not wearing any headgear suggests he has no concern for being identified."

"Does MI5 or MI6 know him?" asked Rupert.

"Apparently not, Prime Minister," answered the head of MI5. "He's an unknown, somehow he's managed to pull a group together and stayed off our radar. Frankly, the most dangerous sort. Which makes the fact he's perfectly happy for his face to be everywhere that much more disconcerting."

The Admiral was keen to understand what, if any, conclusions had been reached. "Where's this all leading, Jessica?"

"Can't be sure, but what we've come up with is as follows. Firstly, the leader is not expecting to come out of this mission alive. He's made no effort to conceal his identity and in his chosen line of work that just makes no sense. Secondly, the men with him are all wearing masks."

"So we have a difference of anticipated end results?" offered Rupert.

"It would seem so, Prime Minister. Further, there has been no great long ideological ranting by the leader; in my opinion he's simply there to kill as many people as possible. The rest of the group, we suspect, is more interested in the promise of a $5bn haul of diamonds," she explained.

"So what about the explosives, if you're right about that?" asked the Admiral.

Jessica continued to lay out her thinking. "Again it's speculation, but there is no obvious way for the group to get out of that building. So if the explosives are not there for the hostages then they have something to do with and escape plan ..."

Rupert filled in some of the gaps. "... An escape plan which the leader of the group has no interest in but the rest of the group clearly does."

"Quite right, so we believe our man Alex spins a story to his men that there is a way out using the explosives in some way, but in reality he plans to blow the whole place up." The heads of MI5 paused and looked at the two men. "In my opinion we need to get in there as quickly as possible. Alex is only interested in some publicity and then blowing everyone, including himself and his team, to kingdom come."

Control Room, News 24 - 16.55

"Time to go to work, Patrick," said Max.

"Agreed," came the reply from the former Special Forces operative.

Both men had witnessed the brutal murder and listened to Alex's rantings. Unspoken, both had already worked out that there would be no negotiation with these terrorists and that to all intents and purposes, unless the group could be talked out of the building, this was going to end in a murderous fire fight.

The guard who had been left to watch over Jerry and his 'essential' skeleton crew in the control room stood at the back of the room and had been chain smoking to pass the time. He was carrying an AK47 and wasn't expecting any acts of heroism from a couple of TV engineers.

Max stood up from the console and walked towards the guard. "I need to go to the toilet."

"Piss in the corner, mate," came the south London laced accent. Max crossed the small room and started to unbutton his jeans; the guard's attention was momentarily distracted as he watched Max. This was all that Patrick needed; he was up and out of his chair. He grabbed the terrorist from behind, choking off any cries for help with his right forearm across the windpipe. At the same time he used his left arm to powerfully twist the man's neck. Everyone in the small room heard the bones crack. The spinal cord was severed and Grant, the one-time guard, fell to the floor dead.

Max pulled out his mobile phone. "Admiral? It's Max." He provided a brief update of their situation.

"When are you sending in the troops?" asked Max. He had no hesitation in believing that this was the only viable option. Alex clearly had no interest in protracted negotiations.

The Admiral checked his watch. "Ten minutes or so. We're going to cut all the power and that'll be the sign for the fire teams. How many terrorists are there?"

"Not exactly sure, but would estimate between fifteen and seventeen in total," replied Max setting the dial on his dive watch. "What do you want us to do?"

"We can handle getting through the doors." The Admiral went on to say, "the big concern is for all the people in the newsroom itself. We start coming through the front door and get held up, we're not going to be able to get to them very quickly. Can you confirm the situation in the newsroom itself?"

"There don't appear to be any bombs rigged, looks like they're working on the basis that they've got them covered with seven or eight heavily armed guards," replied Max.

"Understood," confirmed the Admiral. "Max, we believe that the terrorists DID bring an amount of explosives in with them. What we don't know is where it is and what their intentions are. Our best guess is that Alex plans to blow up the whole building."

"We'll make our way towards the newsroom and clear out what we can on the way. When you cut the power is there going to be any emergency lighting, or is it all going to go dark?" checked Max.

"There will be low emission emergency lights, on their own battery operated circuits so we can't cut them," was the response.

"Understood, we'll get cracking our end."Max was about to cut the call but added, "What about Lockton and his daughter? If we're in the newsroom we're not going to be able to stop someone setting the vest off."

"I know. Good luck, Max." The Admiral cut the call. He didn't have a palatable answer for the very valid point that Max had made.

Max quickly briefed Patrick on the details that the Admiral had imparted.

Max turned to the studio director. "Jerry, you stay here and keep your head down."

"Fuck that, I'm coming with you guys!" came the somewhat unexpected retort.

"Look, mate, it's going to be very dangerous and you could easily get yourself killed," said Patrick.

Jerry was up and heading for the door. "Did you see what that bastard did to Beth? I want to kill every one of these shits."

"Do you know how to shoot?" Patrick asked in a friendly tone.

"Point and pull the trigger, right? Can't be that hard," Jerry replied.

"That's about it Jerry, you're a brave man," said Max with a smile. He picked up AK47 from the fallen guard. Jerry stepped forward to take the rifle. "No mate, I think I'll give you my pistol, less to worry about. And as you say," he pulled out the SIG and put a bullet in the chamber, "point and pull the trigger."

Patrick took point and led the three of them into the corridor behind the control room. Max was bringing up the rear. "Which way to the newsroom, Jerry?" he asked.

"Take a left and then we've got to go down a half flight of stairs. At the bottom you take a sharp right, it'll take us to the big open plan area," replied Jerry.

~

The British government acted quickly and with a single voice. They did not negotiate with terrorists. Instructions were issued quickly and the building on the South Bank was rapidly encircled by heavily armed police and Special Forces soldiers. Since the IRA bombings several decades earlier, the British had always kept a squad of highly trained specialist counter insurgent operatives on 24/7 call.

Outside the building, Greg was giving a final briefing to his fire team Alpha. His group was to go in through the main entrance. Delta, Echo and Gamma fire teams were lined up to hit the other main entrances. He checked his watch: three minutes to go.

~

Max's small band had made their way to the top of the short flight of stairs. He checked his watch. "Jerry, you follow us down, no heroics, got it?" He checked his watch: any second now.

The corridor went dark. A couple of seconds later, as their eyes adjusted, the emergency lighting did its work and they could see their way forward.

Four loud detonations could be heard reverberating around the building. "Go!" shouted Max.

Patrick and Max raced down the stairs followed by Jerry, heavy prolonged gunfire now replacing the loud series of explosions. Taking a sharp right at the bottom of the stairs they exploded into the open plan space that was the newsroom. The screens that would normally be flashing breaking news or being used to compile new material from around the world, sat on the desks dotted around the room, were now all dead. Instead of being met by the normally bright and airy vaulted newsroom, there was only a dull red tinge to the room provided from the emergency lights set in the ceiling and the walls.

In the centre of the room the hostages were sitting, some now screaming in blind panic. The terrorists were taken slightly by surprise when the lights had suddenly gone off and weren't sure what they ought to do. Max and Patrick had no such doubt or hesitation and stormed into the room, firing off crisp individual rounds into the armed men dotted around the room.

The noise was deafening as the defenders began to return fire at the men coming into the room. The muzzle flashes lit up the space above the ambience created by the emergency lights, throwing ghostly shadows against the walls. For the untrained, the scene was totally alien, incredibly frightening and fortunately caused most to freeze where they sat on the floor. "Stay down!" Max ordered. Those that stood risked being confused for active participants in the fire fight, or could simply be caught in the cross fire.

Max and Patrick split up, each taking one side of the room, and laid down a merciless stream of steady lethal fire. Jerry crouched behind a desk and fired in the general direction of where he thought the terrorists were. He would recount later, at great length, that he had definitely personally accounted for four or five of the mercenaries. Something which the survivors were happy not to correct; they were impressed with the man's undoubted bravery. His marksmanship skills left a little to be desired.

Three or four minutes into the fire fight, half of the terrorists were down, professionals versus amateurs accounting for the one-sided casualty figures. From what Max could see across the room, now filling with cordite from the rounds being exchanged, only a couple of the hostages had been hit in the mêlée.

Through one of the doors on the far side of the newsroom Alpha team, led by Greg, entered the fray. Max looked around the room for Alex: no sign. "Patrick, Greg," he shouted across the room "You guys wrap this up, I'm going to the studio."

Max made his way back the way he had come and, leaving the newsroom running at full speed, headed for the studio. He covered the distance in less than ninety seconds.

The TV studio was bathed in a ghostly light. A mixture of emergency floor lighting and the now infrequent flash of gunfire combining with the dull glow coming from the newsroom behind the glass panel that made up the backdrop to the studio. Max cautiously made his way, keeping to the shadows where possible, towards the centre of the room.

Alex was standing behind Jo with a gun pointed at her head. In front of them both stood Lord Lockton with his back to Max.

"Let her go, Alex." The Lord wasn't begging, he was asking in a level tone of voice as if to indicate that everyone knew that it was all over, and what would be the point of killing his daughter?

"Shut up, old man. I'm going to shoot her and then kill you too," snarled Alex.

"Daddy, I'm so very sorry." Jo was in tears.

"I know, and so am I. I blame myself for what you have become. It's all my fault, please forgive me Josephine." The father understood that he must share at least part of the blame. She was his daughter and ultimately his responsibility; he had always loved her but had never learnt how to show it properly.

The look between them, as Alex cocked the pistol that he had pressed against Jo's temple, bridged the gap of decades and they became father and daughter once again.

"How sweet," hissed Alex and tightened his finger on the trigger. Just as he was about to blow her brains out, Alex saw Max entering the scene over Jo's father's shoulder . "Who the hell are you?" demanded the terrorist.

Max had his rifle pointed directly at Alex's head; the weapon was held steady and he knew his aim would be true. He had learned many years ago that it was pointless to argue with a fool, especially one waving a gun around. Gently exhaling, he pulled the trigger. The bullet smashed into Alex's forehead removing most of the back of his skull and killing him instantly in the process. The look of shock and surprise on his face as he fell backwards was almost comical.

"Jo, get yourself and your father out of the building now," commanded Max.

Jo looked like a rabbit caught in the full beam of a car's headlights. She was clearly in a state of shock, and froze. Max grabbed the TV presenter and pushed her in the general direction of the studio door. "Looks like it's down to you, Lord Lockton, get her and yourself out. We reckon there might be a bomb somewhere in the building."

"Thank you," Jo's father said, tearing off the suicide vest, as he passed Max and dragged Jo behind him to where he guessed he might find an exit to the building.

Max raced back downstairs to find Patrick and Greg assisting in herding the very scared hostages out of the building. He took a quick look around the room; power had now been restored and he could see half a dozen of the terrorists lying where they had fallen. The Special Forces troops had seven or eight men at gunpoint and were driving them out behind the newsroom staff.

It was going to take another good ten minutes or so to clear the area. "Where's the bomb?" asked Max of his two team members. "Not here, boss," said Greg.

"Fuck, for all we know it could go off any second." Max sprinted over to where some of Alex's men were about to be led away. Going up to the nearest mercenary, he said, "Where's the bomb?"

"Go fuck yourself, pal."

Max smashed the man's face with the butt of the AK47, his face disintegrated into a mess of broken teeth, flattened nose and all nicely framed with copious amounts of blood. He went to the next man under arrest. "Where's the bomb?" The man knew that Max wasn't fooling around and frankly saw little point in getting a rifle smashed into his, albeit less than 'movie star' quality, visage.

"Data centre, downstairs," came the swift, fear-inspired response.

"Which way?" demanded Max, the mercenary pointed towards some doors off to the left of where they were standing.

Max covered the distance in double quick time, crashing through the door he found a staircase leading into the bowels of the building. Taking the steps in massive leaps, he ended up in a small concrete floored hall area which had several doors leading off to various technical service areas. "Fuck which way now?" muttered Max under his breath.

"Looks like you could do with a bit of help." Unbeknown to Max, in his headlong rush down the stairs he had been followed by Jerry, the brave and somewhat out of breath studio director.

"You're a star mate, which way to the data centre?" asked Max.

"This way." Jerry led him a little way down the concrete floored hall and then opened a door on their right. The room was full of servers and telecoms equipment. It reminded Max of something one might see on an episode of Star Trek.

In the middle of the room next to what looked like a bank of routers was a pile of bags; sitting adjacent on a small desk and connected by a multitude of cables was what looked like the detonator. The digital clock indicated they had less than a minute to deactivate the device. Max went over to take a better look. -48- read the digital display. *Jesus, what cable am I supposed to pull out?*

-43-

"Know anything about bombs, Jerry?" quipped Max.

-37-

"You must be fucking kidding mate, I thought you were the expert." He was beginning to regret not having bolted for freedom with everyone else.

Here goes nothing, thought Max as he grabbed a bunch of cables connected to the device; he was about to pull out the wires

-27-

when he was knocked off his feet by Patrick giving him a heavy shoulder charge.

-21-

Max lay on the floor and looked up at Patrick.

-17-

"Sometimes, Max, I despair of you."

-14-

Patrick nonchalantly picked up the device and turned it upside down.

-11-

"See," he turned an almost totally hidden dial on the back. "Easy when you know how."

The clock stopped at -6-.

Patrick proceeded to pull all the wires out of the detonator and lobbed it playfully in Max's direction. "Haven't seen one of those for a few years," he said with a smile.

Epilogue

The final body count of the innocents killed in the newsroom came to eight; another dozen would be in hospital for a few days or a couple of weeks depending on the severity of their injuries. In the end, eight of the mercenary group had been arrested. As suspected, they were there mainly for the money, a mixed band of small-time hoods from across Europe and further afield: a real international band.

FAUKSUR was added to the list of terrorist groups that unfortunately populate society.

Max, Patrick and Greg were sitting in a pub just down the road from the office in Chiswick, enjoying a Friday night after-work drink. Max was only for a quick one as he was looking forward to meeting up with Gina in the West End later that evening. They were getting together supposedly for a debrief on the whole sorry business, but both were secretly hoping that the work element could be kept to a minimum and they could look forward to a nice evening out together.

Patrick had pointed out to Max and Greg that, in all likelihood, they were unlikely to hear from this 'new' group again.

"My view is that Alex put this whole business together to show how easy it was to have a go at his favourite targets." The autopsy on what remained of Alex's head would later reveal the inoperable brain tumour.

"How do you know that? It could have been Germany, Russia or whomever," asked Max.

"Then he would have had to come up with another name," replied Patrick.

"How so?" Max was intrigued to know what Patrick had come up with this time.

"It came to me this morning. FAUKSUR is an anagram of UK, USA and FR. This was a virtual terrorist organisation brought together from a bunch of smaller disparate groups," observed Patrick.

"So you're saying that they never really had a common cause?" asked Greg.

"That would be my view; they all had an axe to grind. Easy enough to find some loose common ground or cause, and very straight forward to pick some targets," confirmed Patrick.

Max could see where Patrick's thought process was leading. "Well, if you're right, that's very worrying Patrick. Follow your logic through and we'll see any number of groups forming and dissolving almost on a whim."

"You've got it. Living in such a connected world it's easy to find people who share similar rabid views." Patrick was curious about Jo's fate. "What happened to Jo Lockton, I guess she won't be doing many more TV programmes in the near future?"

"They've put her in solitary at Belmarsh for the time being," answered Max.

"After what she's done she's not going last long in the open population," mused Greg.

"No, she's not," confirmed Max.

Authors note:

The Max Thatcher Series

Thank you for reading Without Warning. If you have, as I would hope, enjoyed this story then you would most likely be entertained by Gatekeeper, which was my first book, and the Platinum Solution, the second in the Max Thatcher Series.

Gatekeeper

Prologue

French Airspace - Wednesday Night

Flight BA487 had left Heathrow on time, bound for Dubai. The flight was busy; it always was, Dubai being a very popular holiday attraction in its own right and one which had also, over the last ten years, established itself as a major hub for the near and far East, providing frequent connecting routes into every major business city and favoured tourist location.

Susan sat in the economy section of the Boeing 777 looking forward to getting to Dubai for a bit of shopping. She'd never been there, but her friends had been told stories of wondrous shops with knock-down prices. A supersized Harrods in a series of fabulously clean, perfectly air-conditioned terminal buildings – a great way to spend a couple of hours waiting for her connecting Emirates flight on to Sydney.

She was so looking forward to a month of travelling; she'd spent hours doing research on the internet. On the advice of more seasoned travellers, Susan had written a long list of 'must dos'. As this was her first major long-haul trip on her own, she was hoping to meet up with some like-minded fun people to share all her new and exciting experiences.

She had broken up with Marty, her boyfriend of three years, a couple of weeks earlier. He had wanted a serious commitment – two-point-four kids and a nice house in suburbia. Susan felt this was all a little bit too premature. They'd argued, she'd walked out and now she was on her way towards a bit of adventure. In her own mind she was pretty certain that the two of them would work things out when she got back; but in the interim this was her life, to be lived to the full, and at 23 the petite brunette felt she was entitled to some fun before settling down to a life of matrimonial and domestic bliss.

Susan played with the entertainment controls and settled back to watch a movie. *Love, Lost and Found* had just come out featuring her favourite actress, Sally Stevens, with the bonus of having the gorgeous and oh-so-sexy George Hadley playing opposite her. Her last rom-com had been great fun and according to the reviews that she had read in the Evening Standard on her daily commute back from the smog of Central London, this movie was a good laugh. It had everything by all accounts; a great storyline, lots of intrigue, with some twists and turns in the plot thrown in for good measure. Headphones on, movie starting and looking forward to a couple of drinkies – life was good.

She never got past the opening scene, as the BA487 ploughed straight into the Air France 290 coming out of Paris bound for Atlanta. At 20,000 feet, over the killing fields of Flanders, the planes collided and erupted in a single massive ball of flame; there would be metal debris spread over a 100-mile radius below to be picked over and collected by the air investigators. For the friends and families of the 700-odd passengers and crew on both flights there would be no remains to bury, only the hollow consolation that the ashes of their loved ones would be scattered amongst the poppies, along with so many that had sacrificed their lives in the Great War **The**

Platinum Solution

Prologue

Gans Baai, Western Cape South Africa – Monday, Early Morning

Gordon, a landlubber at heart, was feeling sick to the core. It wasn't simply the motion of the boat lolling around in the 3ft swell, which didn't help, but the knowledge that he was in a lot of trouble. Why hadn't he kept his mouth shut and just gone along with the whole crazy scheme? He cursed himself for the thousandth time. *Shit, I should have known better*, he thought.

Henk turned to look at the man dressed in a badly sweat stained business shirt and slacks, hands tied, lying helpless in the well of the boat; he was rather looking forward to this morning's entertainment. A mile away he could see the small harbour at Gans Baai which would be a hive of activity later in the day when the tourists came to get scared by the local attractions. Turning to face the front of the 30ft former commercial fishing boat constructed out of wood and fiberglass, he could see their destination about fifteen minutes ahead. Small waves were breaking between Dyer Island and Geyser Rock, the smaller of the two islands. These rocky outcrops provided a permanent home to over 60,000 resident cape fur seals. The smell of guano filled the nostrils of those on board; later in the day, under the full glare of the summer sun, the smell would become almost overpowering.

The weather was pretty unremarkable that morning, the sky was overcast, early teens showing on the boats thermometer; the mid-summer sun had not yet done its work and burnt off the grey mantle of cloud that hung over the bay.

"Let's head for the gap in the channel," he called up to the skipper – a member of the Fraternity who could be trusted to keep schtum about the morning's proposed proceedings. He was a good man in Henk's eyes, and another committed believer in the 'great cause.'

"Sure, no problem."

"Henk, for Pete's sake, we can work this out. It's really not a problem; I can get back onto London and sort this misunderstanding out."

"Too late for that, Gordon. You knew the rules, your bank balance confirms that we kept our side of the bargain; you're a very foolish man thinking that you could blackmail us. See what happens if you get too greedy? The Fraternity looks after its friends and punishes its enemies."

The steady hum of the engine changed its beat as the boat slowed down to a walking pace from the steady 12 knots that it had been making across the open water.

"Look, I'll give you all the money back, you'll never hear from me again – I'll take my family and disappear." A slight grin appeared across Henk's heavy-built facial features; at 6ft 2in he was a big man. He was dressed in his preferred attire of camouflage trousers, army boots and cut-off green T shirt. Weighing in at over 18 stone, he'd played a lot of rugby as a boy in the privileged private all-white schooling system that he had enjoyed. Growing up in a wealthy Afrikaans family, he had been used to the better things in life. Staff to look after the gardens and the inherited farm, a career mapped out in the family business – all good.

But over time life had changed; with the departure of Apartheid, all of a sudden he was supposed to become acclimatised to treating the blacks as equals. Positive discrimination had led to having to employ non-whites in positions of influence within the business, and what had once been a private 'by invitation only' club was now becoming, at a frightening pace, open to all and frankly that didn't sit very well with him or many of his peers.

No, in his mind things had gone too far, something had to be done. "Gordon, save your breath. You're past redemption, if I were you I would concentrate on making your peace with God." With that, he gave the defenceless man a solid kick in the midriff on the basis that would stop any further pointless discussion.

The boat's skipper, Pieter, pointed the *Cape Fisher* into the swell and cut the engine. There was no tide running to speak of and in the light chop he knew an anchor wasn't required as the boat wouldn't move far off its current position. Coming out of the cabin he looked across at Henk; "What's the plan? Shall we put a bit of hors d'oeuvres out there and see what's around?" In his early 50s, he'd leapt at the chance of joining the elite club called the Fraternity. He was not from wealthy stock but was very proud to be Afrikaans by birthright.

"What have you got in mind?" asked Henk. "I rather thought we might have a bit of a troll and see what we catch?" A keen fisherman, he was referring to the process of trailing bait in the water to attract the target fish of the day.

"Sure, whatever, but we can't be out here too long without attracting a bit of attention." Pieter looked to the shore line; he estimated that unless someone had binoculars trained on them they would be fine and pass unnoticed.

The pair decided on a combination of both fish-attracting approaches – lifting the hapless Gordon up between them, Henk got a bait knife and cut deeply into the struggling man's legs. Gordon screamed with pain and begged them to reconsider their chosen course of action. The pair tied a thick rope around the man's already tightly secured wrists. By this time the prisoner was thrashing violently in desperation, knowing full well his likely fate; but all to no avail as he was easily outmuscled and outweighed.

In almost a single movement Gordon, the lead analyst from BDS Bank based on Broad Street in the City of London, was unceremoniously deposited over the side of the boat.

The coldness of the water took his breath away and he had to kick violently to keep from sinking under the weight of his quickly sodden clothes. The wet clothes and weakened legs due to blood loss combined with the inability to use his hands made staying afloat for any length of time only a remote possibility. Henk looked down at the drowning man and pulled playfully on the rope. "How's the water?"

Pieter turned to his left and picked up a small dustbin full of blood and offal that he had secured for the day's fishing from a slaughterhouse some 33 clicks up the road in Hermanus. Situated to the north west, on the main road back towards Cape Town, Hermanus is world renowned as a great place to go and watch migrating whales.

Lifting the lid, he waved the contents under Henk's nose. "Ummm, lovely – fancy some for breakfast?"

"Ag man, get that out of my face, smells awful!"

"Ag, don't be so fussy." Taking the loaded bucket to the gunwale Pieter promptly deposited the contents over the side, much of it covering Gordon who was frantically trying to find some respite by holding onto the boat.

Returning to the cabin, the skipper pushed the fishing boat's throttle forward a single notch and headed towards shark alley, as the gap between the two islands was more commonly known. Henk played out about 20 yards of rope and watched as it tightened up to the 'bait' and then began to drag the City man along in the wake of the boat. A couple of the local cape fur seals popped their heads up off the starboard bow to have a look at what was going on; they weren't going to have to wait for long.

Gordon was fighting for breath, being dragged by the boat. His mouth was continually filling up with salt water and he knew if this went on much longer, he was going to drown. His onetime business associates - but now recent captors - would have been disappointed if a simple matter of drowning was the only fate befalling the man who had come close to scuppering the whole project.

The Carcharodon carcharias that picked up the scent of the blood in the water was a big female; she was in short term residence in one of the most prolific mating areas for her breed in the world. The Great White made so famous by Peter Benchley's 'Jaws' can grow to over 20ft and has no known predators, it's a prehistoric eating machine. This female was at 14ft an awesome specimen. Now in the chum trail comprising the slaughterhouse delicacies mixed with Gordon's blood and urine, she was moving at pace from underneath the trawled 'bait'.

Gordon probably knew nothing of his untimely demise; he had known that when he'd been bundled into the car the night before and deposited in the dawn on the fishing boat that things were not going to end well. He knew well enough what Gans Baai was famous for, and once he had hit the water he had simply prayed for a swift onset of the anticipated terrible bloody conclusion. He had half expected to see his whole life pass before his eyes and to think about the wife and children that he would be leaving behind. None of that took up his thoughts for the last few moments of his life; his whole consciousness was filled with terror of not knowing what it was like to be eaten alive.

The most feared predator of the high seas, one that had almost singlehandedly put millions of people off going for a quick swim, hit the doomed man at some 18 knots. Black soulless eyes rolled back to avoid being damaged; with her cavernous mouth open, lined with razor sharp teeth, she had come in on a slightly tilted attack path. The 2,400lb Great White ripped through Gordon's rib cage and lifted him entirely out of the water as though he were a rag doll. The two men watching from the boat were suitably impressed and delighted in equal measure to have witnessed the attack so up close – one to share with boys at the bar and maybe tell the kids about one day.

Though possibly, with hindsight, they would change the story with regard to what bait had been used, at least for the child friendly version.

Printed in Great Britain
by Amazon.co.uk, Ltd.,
Marston Gate.